P9-DXK-908

EEK & ACK
The Puzzling Pluto Plot

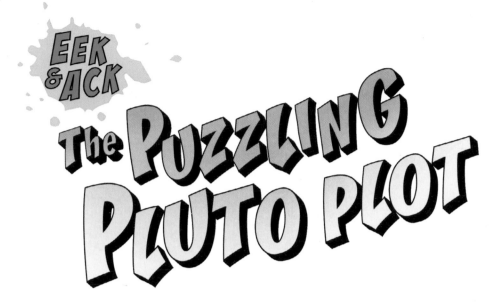

Librarian Reviewer
Katharine Kan
Graphic novel reviewer and Library Consultant, Panama City, FL
MLS in Library and Information Studies, University of Hawaii at Manoa, HI

Reading Consultant
Elizabeth Stedem
Educator/Consultant, Colorado Springs, CO
MA in Elementary Education, University of Denver, CO

STONE ARCH BOOKS
Minneapolis San Diego

Graphic Sparks are published by Stone Arch Books
151 Good Counsel Drive, P.O. Box 669
Mankato, Minnesota 56002
www.stonearchbooks.com

Library of Congress Cataloging-in-Publication Data
Hoena, B. A.
     The Puzzling Pluto Plot / by Blake A. Hoena; illustrated by Steve Harpster.
     p. cm. — (Graphic Sparks—Eek and Ack)
     ISBN 978-1-4342-0452-3 (library binding)
     ISBN 978-1-4342-0502-5 (paperback)
     1. Graphic novels. I. Harpster, Steve. II. Title.
PN6727.H57P89 2008
741.5'973—dc22   2007031255

Summary: Eek and Ack aren't giving up! The Terrible Twosome from the Great Goo
Galaxy are out to conquer Earth once again. But maybe they should have studied up on
the solar system first. Let's just say, the "planet" Pluto will never be the same.

Art Director: Heather Kindseth
Graphic Designer: Brann Garvey

For Curt, who continues to believe
in Pluto's planetary status

1 2 3 4 5 6 13 12 11 10 09 08

Printed in the United States of America

Eek & Ack

The Puzzling Pluto Plot

by Blake A. Hoena

illustrated by Steve Harpster

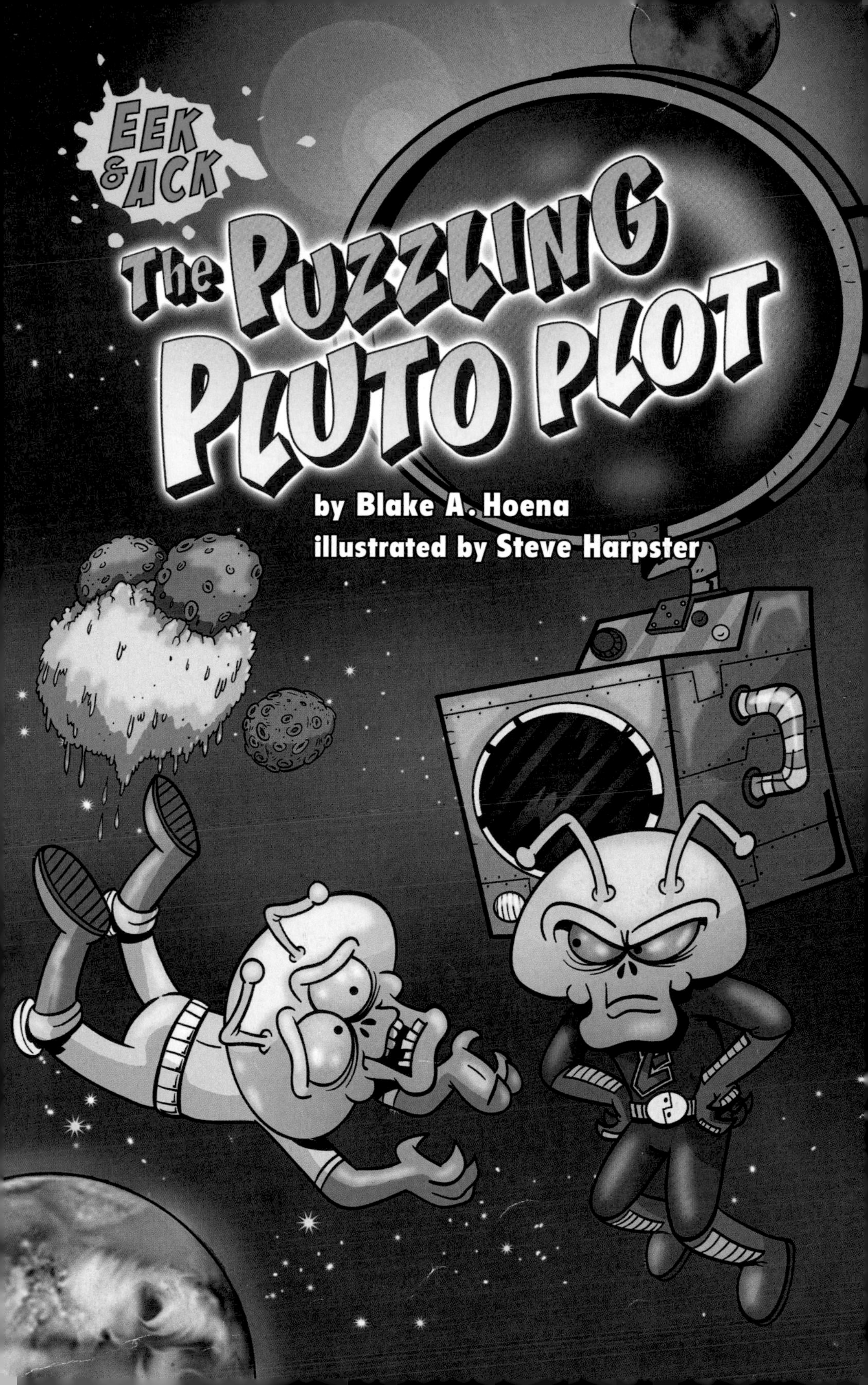

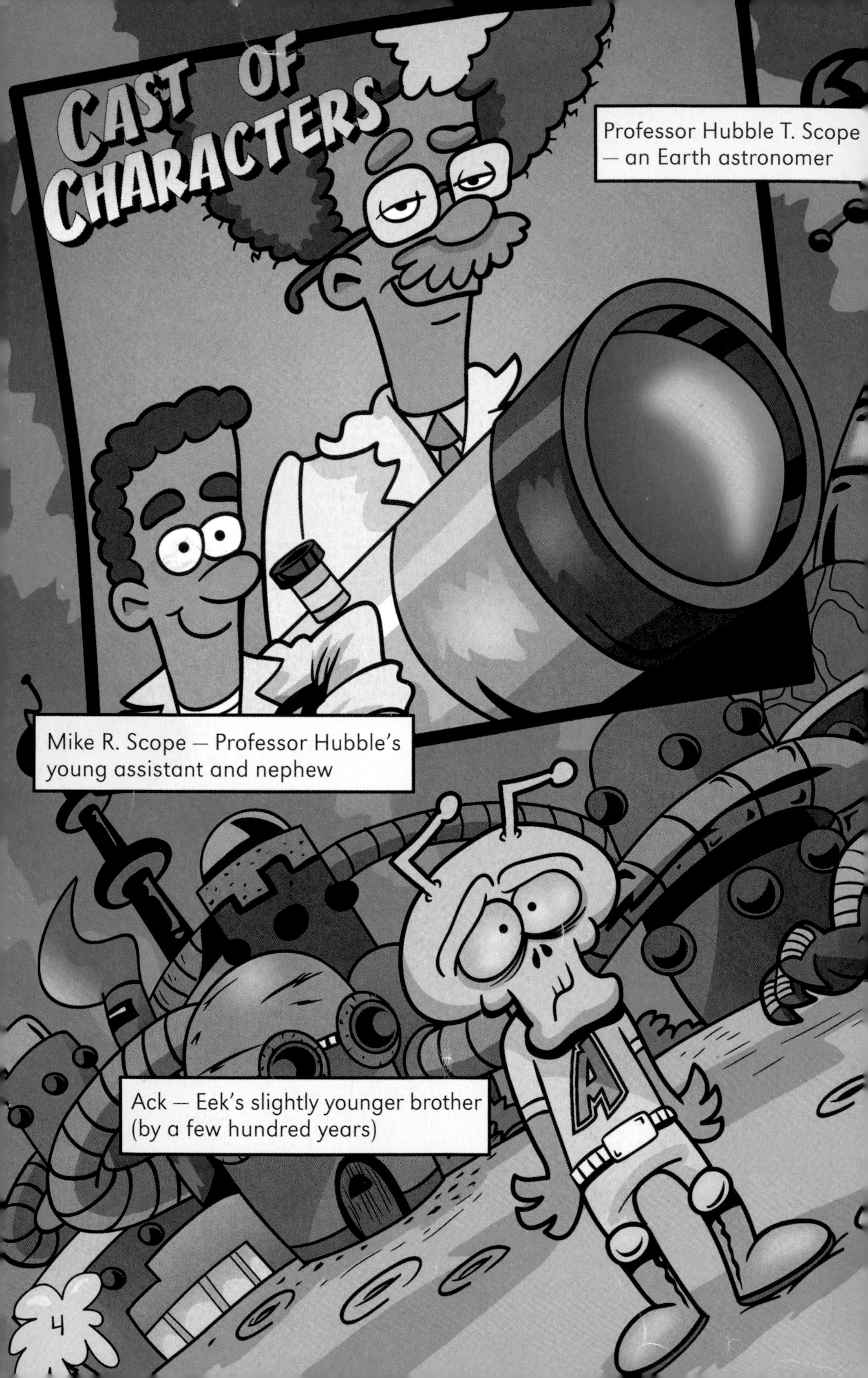
CAST OF CHARACTERS
Professor Hubble T. Scope — an Earth astronomer
Mike R. Scope — Professor Hubble's young assistant and nephew
Ack — Eek's slightly younger brother (by a few hundred years)

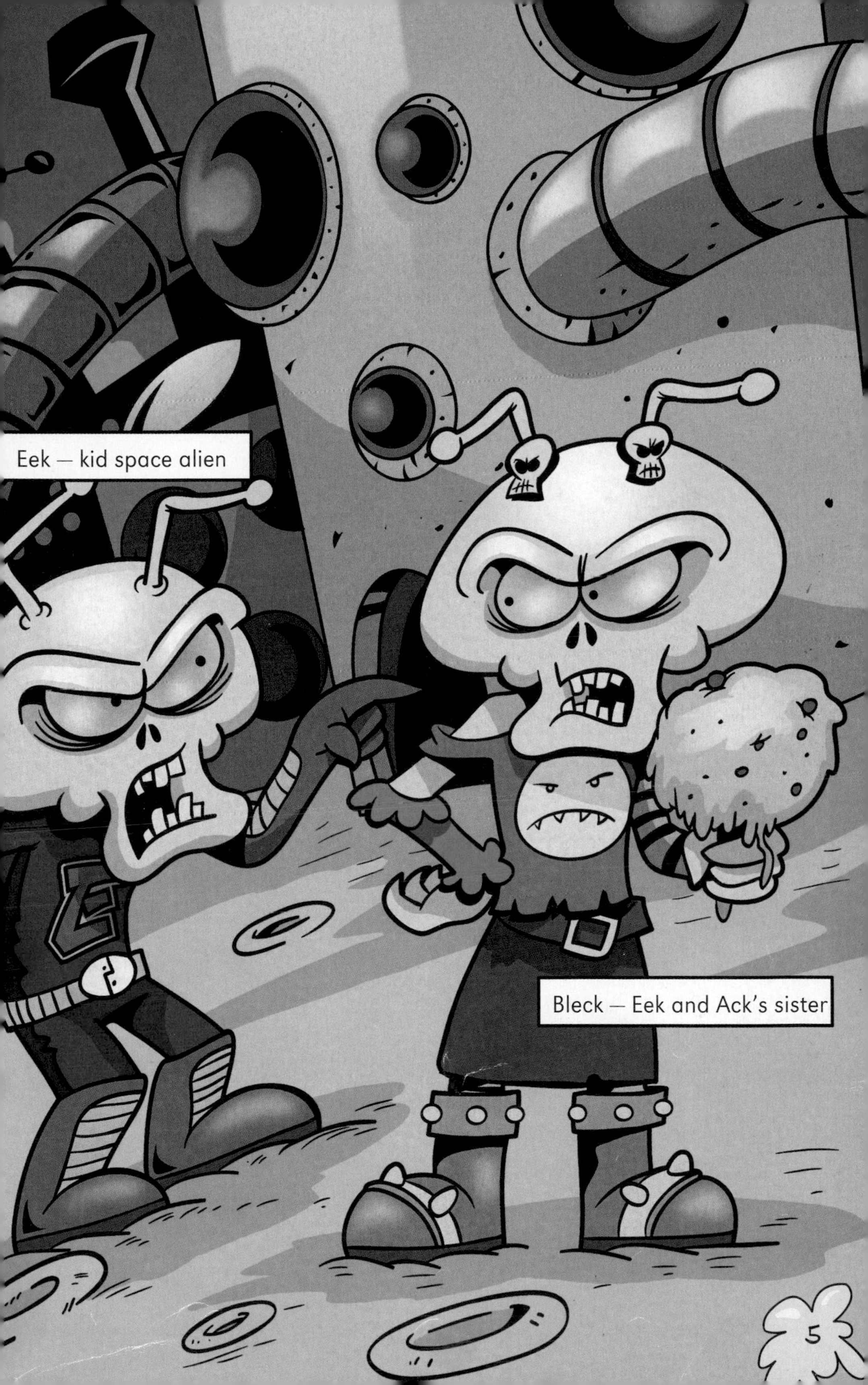
Eek — kid space alien
Bleck — Eek and Ack's sister

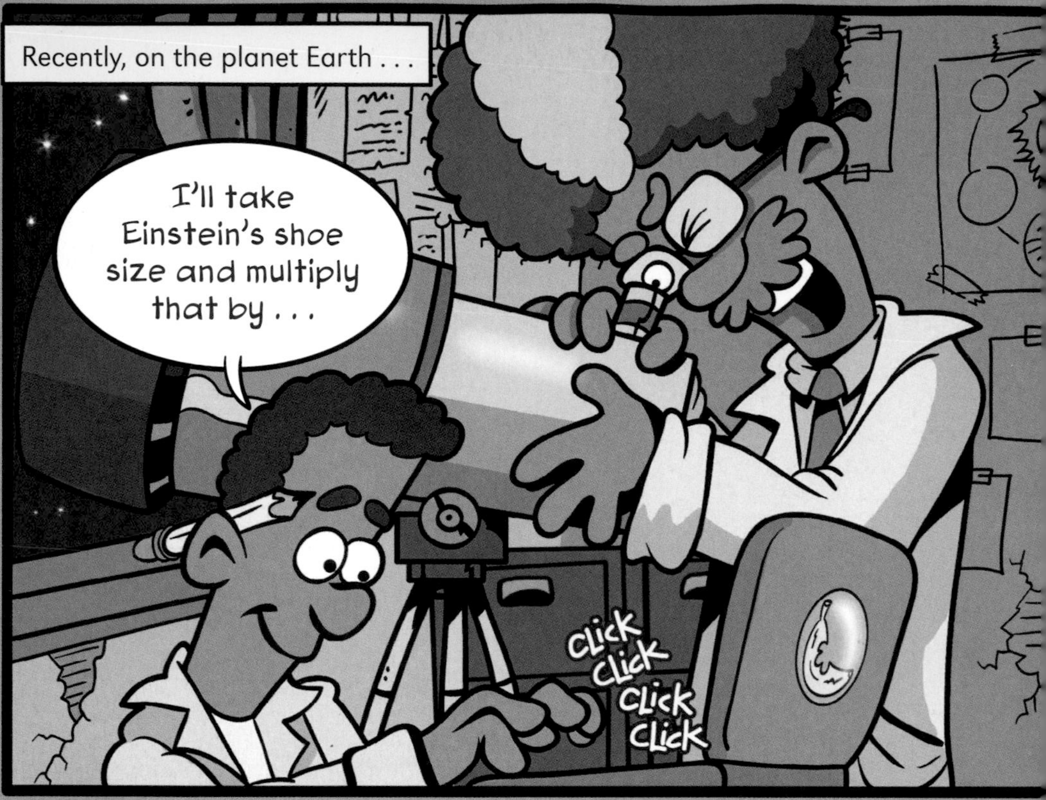
Recently, on the planet Earth . . .
I'll take Einstein's shoe size and multiply that by . . .
CLICK CLICK CLICK CLICK

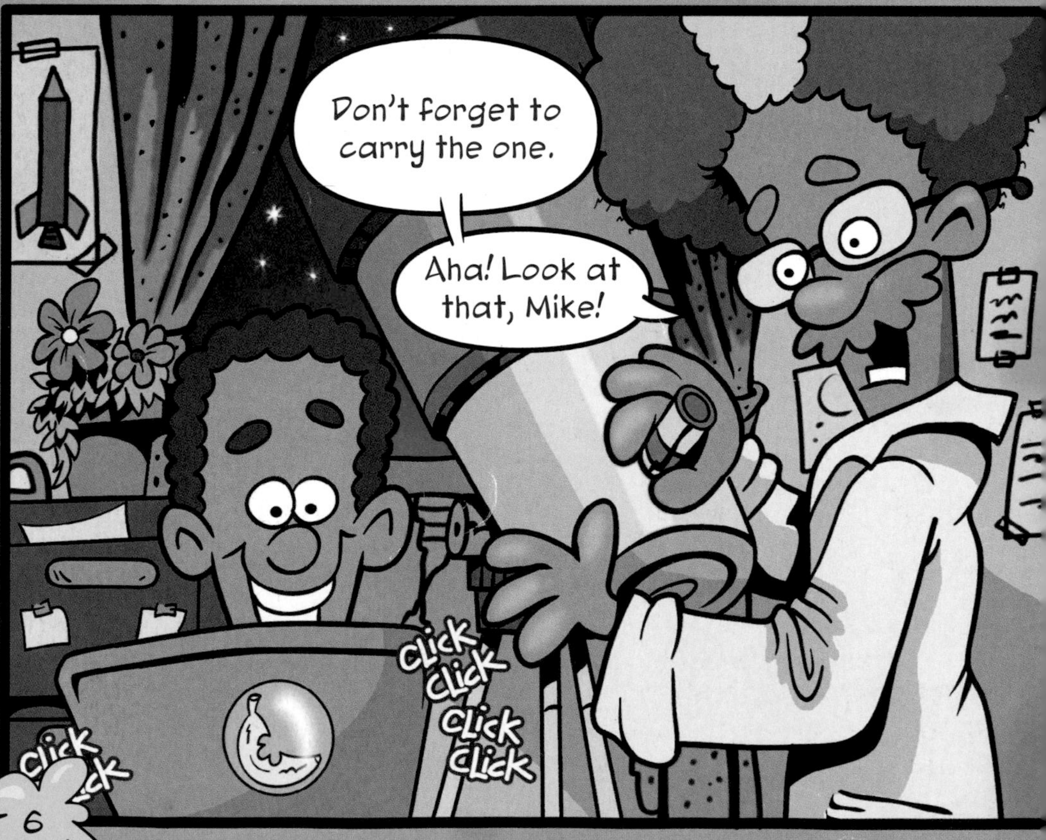
Don't forget to carry the one.
Aha! Look at that, Mike!
CLICK CLICK CLICK CLICK

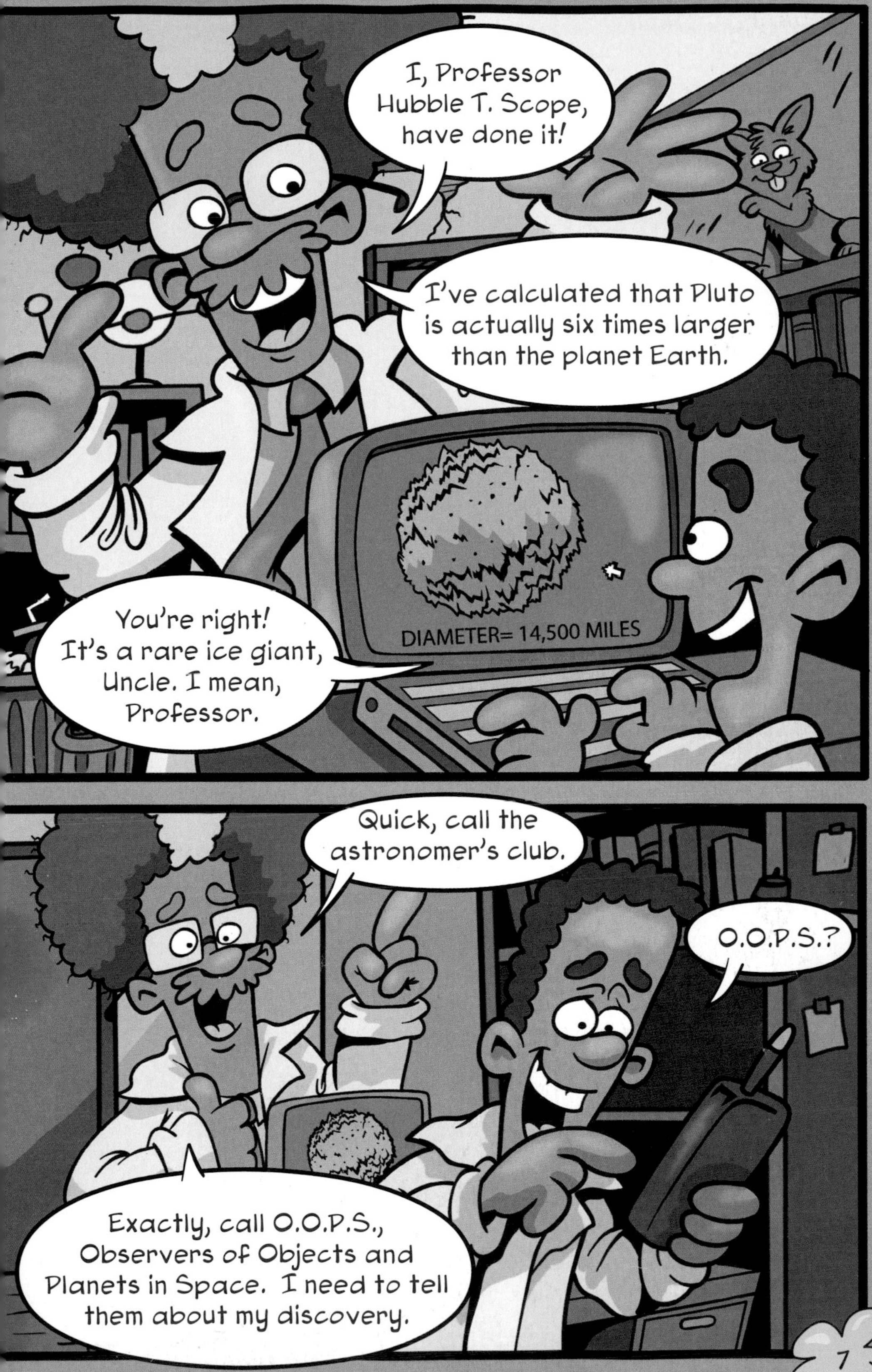
I, Professor Hubble T. Scope, have done it!
I've calculated that Pluto is actually six times larger than the planet Earth.
DIAMETER= 14,500 MILES
You're right! It's a rare ice giant, Uncle. I mean, Professor.
Quick, call the astronomer's club.
O.O.P.S.?
Exactly, call O.O.P.S., Observers of Objects and Planets in Space. I need to tell them about my discovery.

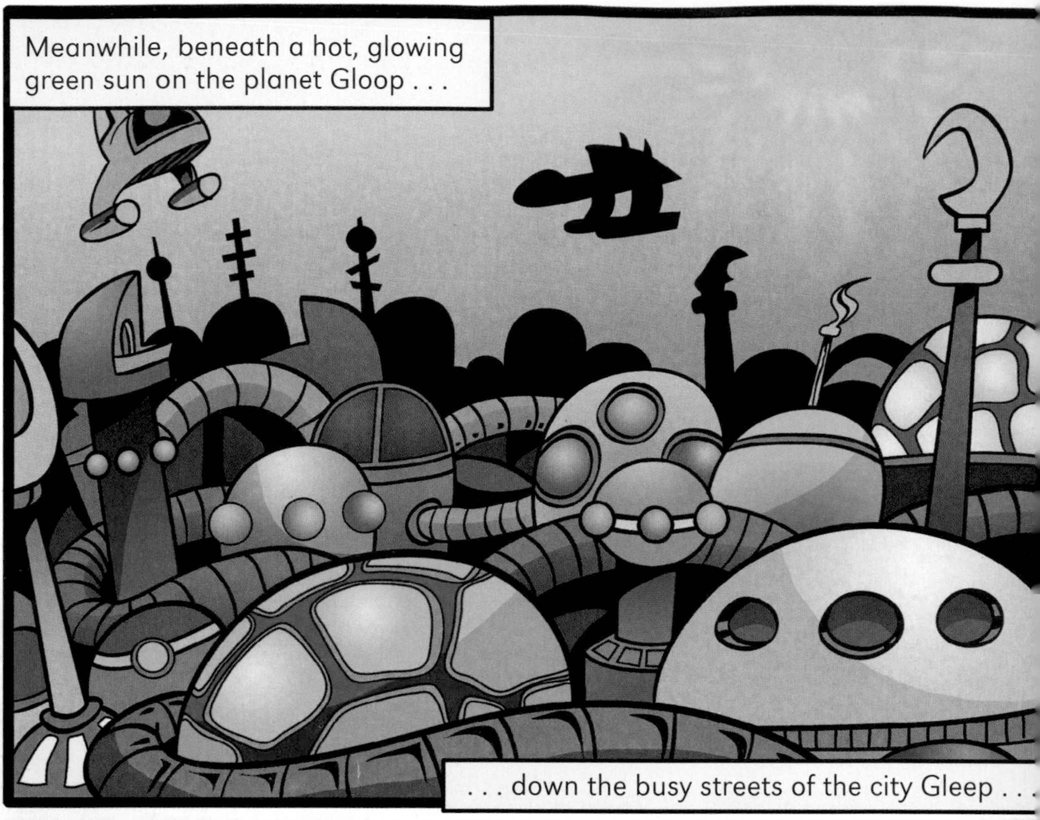
Meanwhile, beneath a hot, glowing green sun on the planet Gloop . . .
. . . down the busy streets of the city Gleep . . .

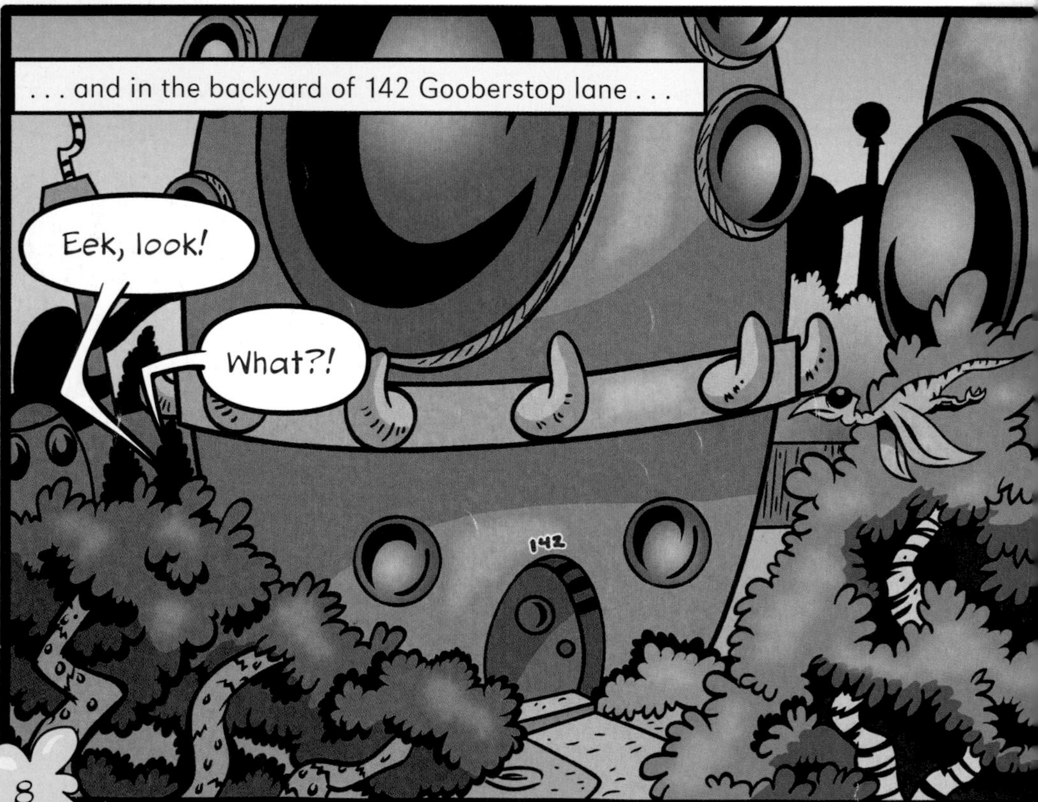
. . . and in the backyard of 142 Gooberstop lane . . .
Eek, look!
What?!
142

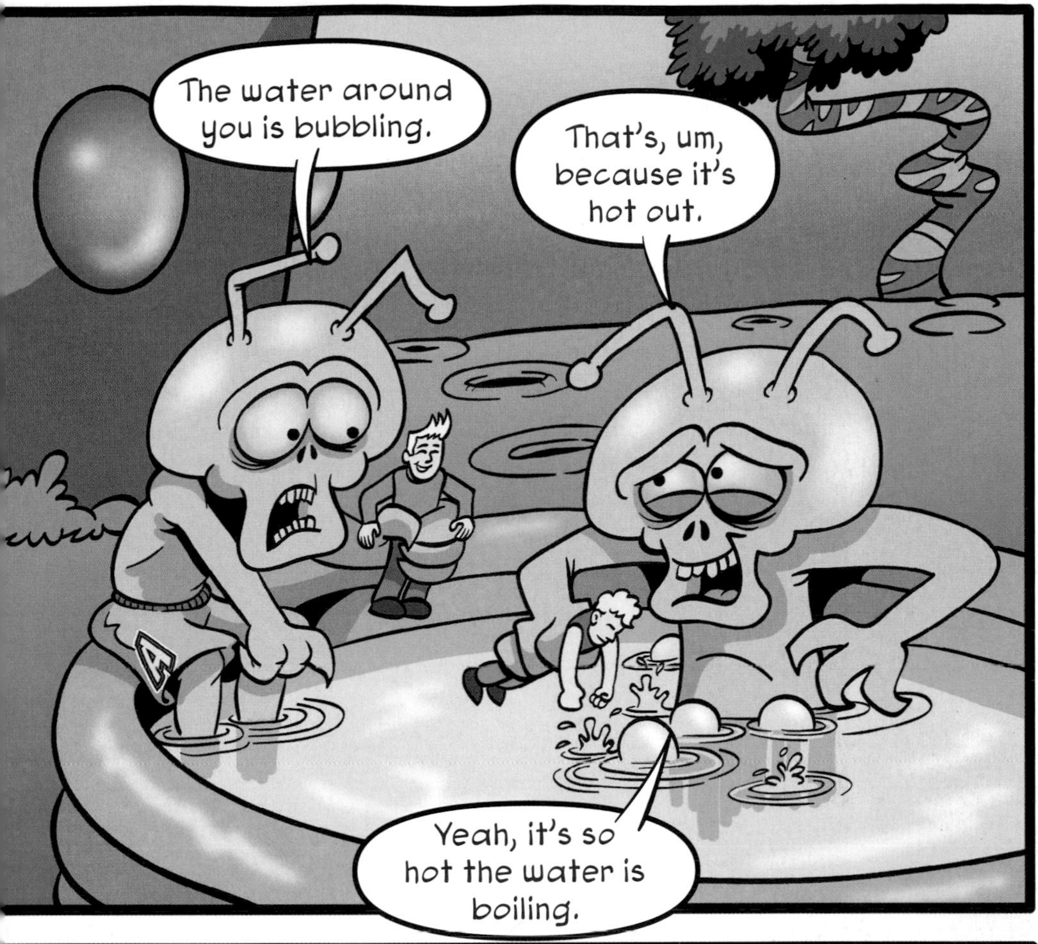
The water around you is bubbling.
That's, um, because it's hot out.
Yeah, it's so hot the water is boiling.

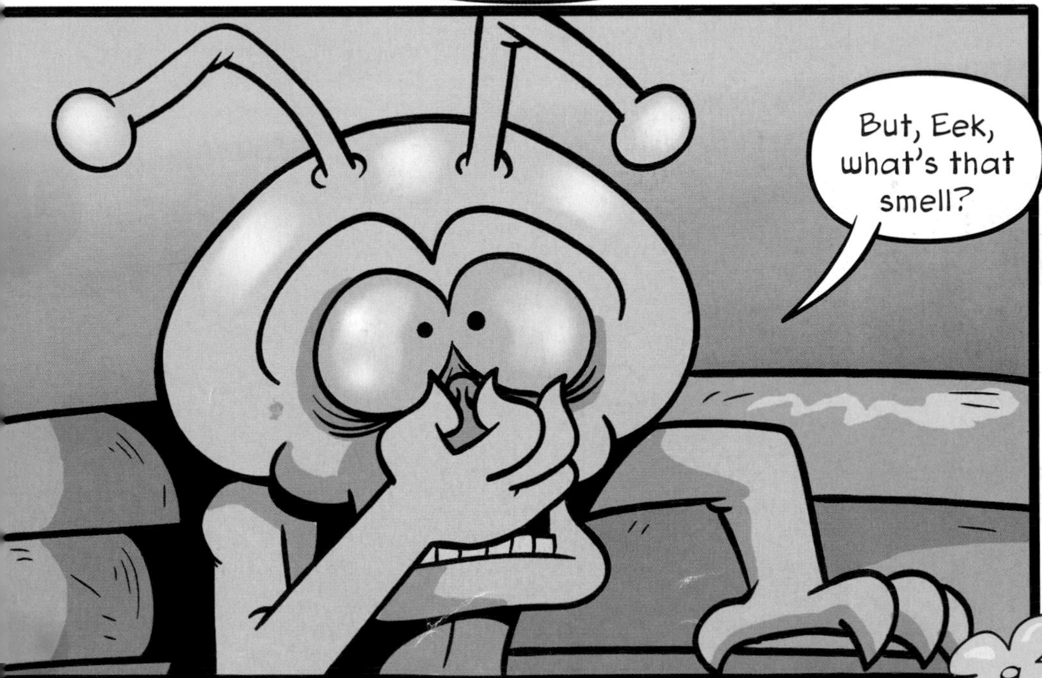
But, Eek, what's that smell?

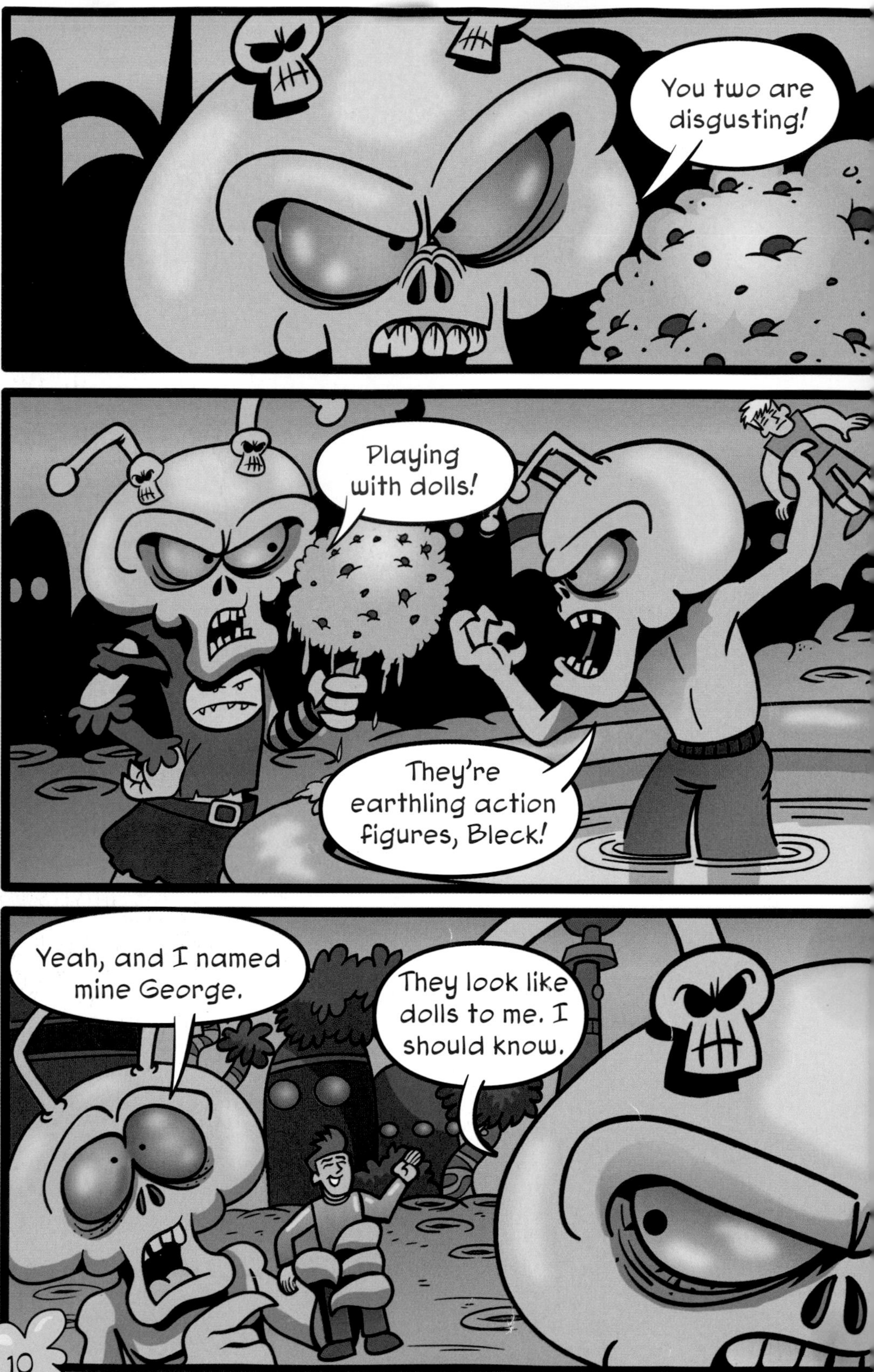
You two are disgusting!
Playing with dolls!
They're earthling action figures, Bleck!
Yeah, and I named mine George.
They look like dolls to me. I should know.

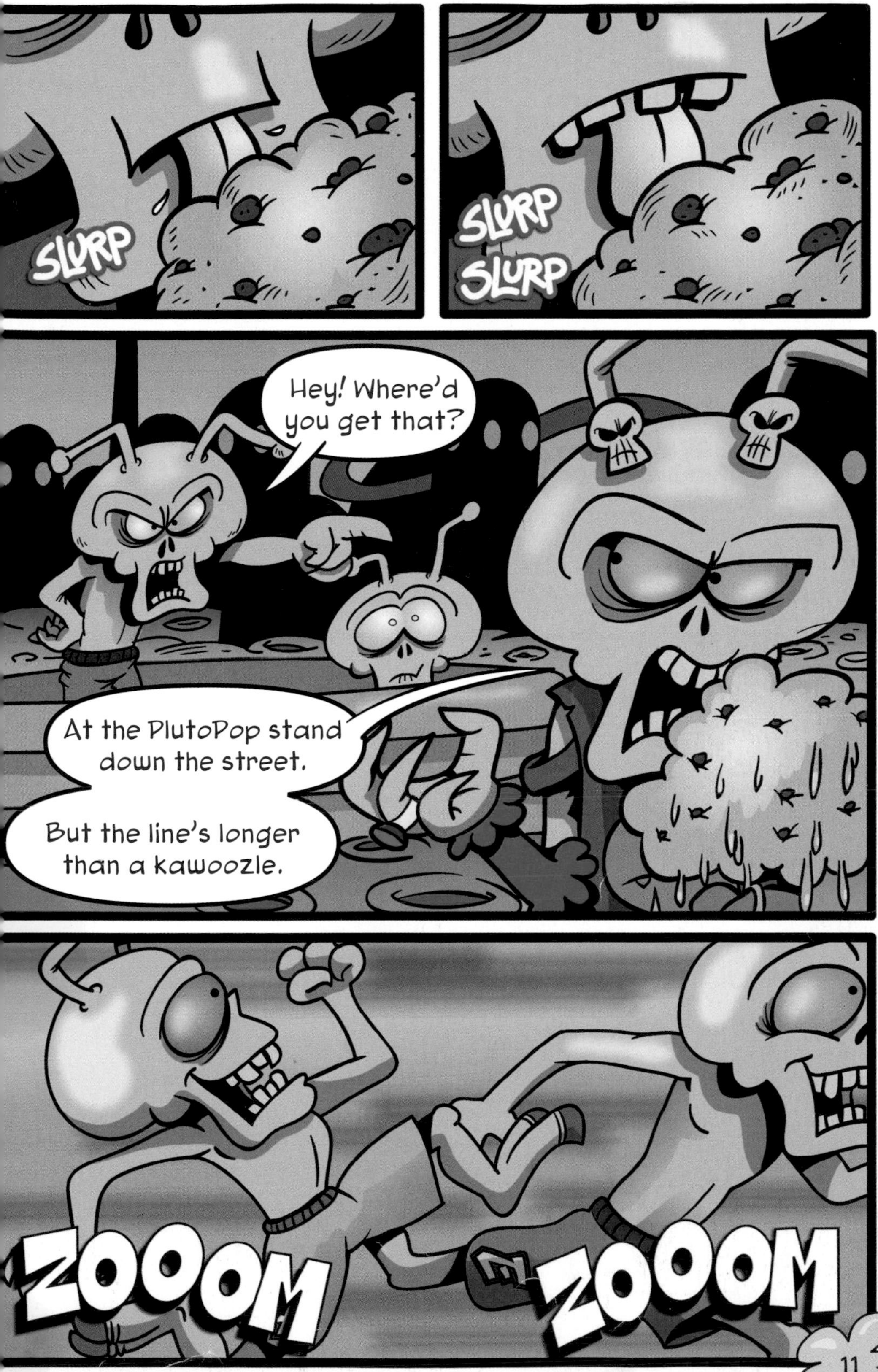
SLURP
SLURP
SLURP
Hey! Where'd you get that?
At the PlutoPop stand down the street.
But the line's longer than a kawoozle.
ZOOOM
ZOOOM

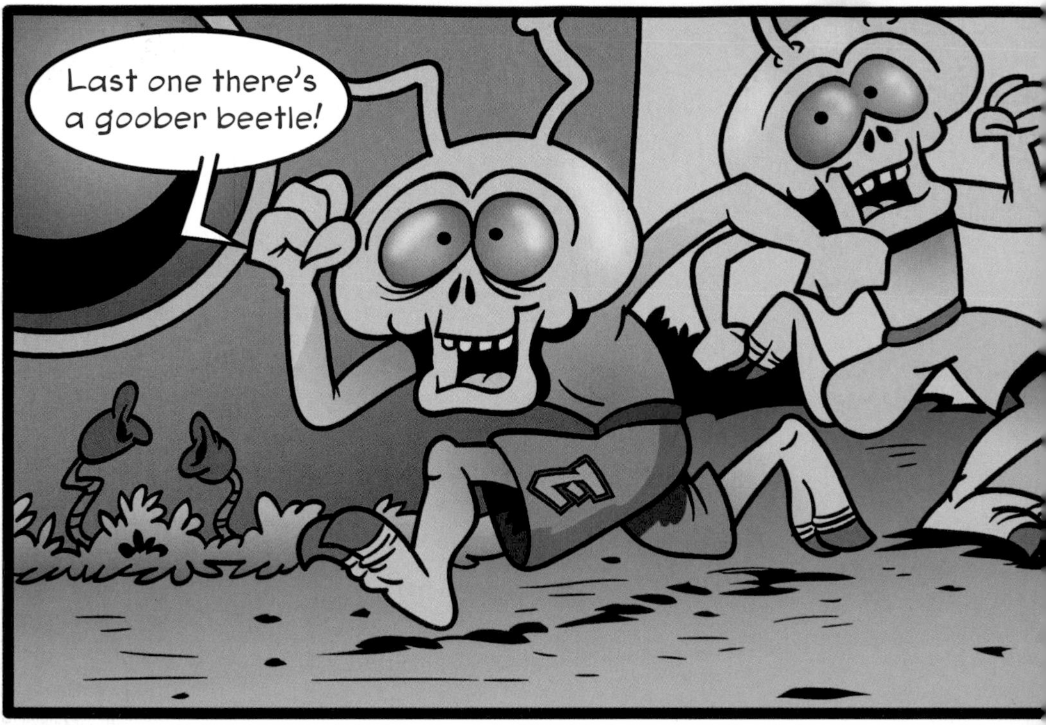
Last one there's a goober beetle!

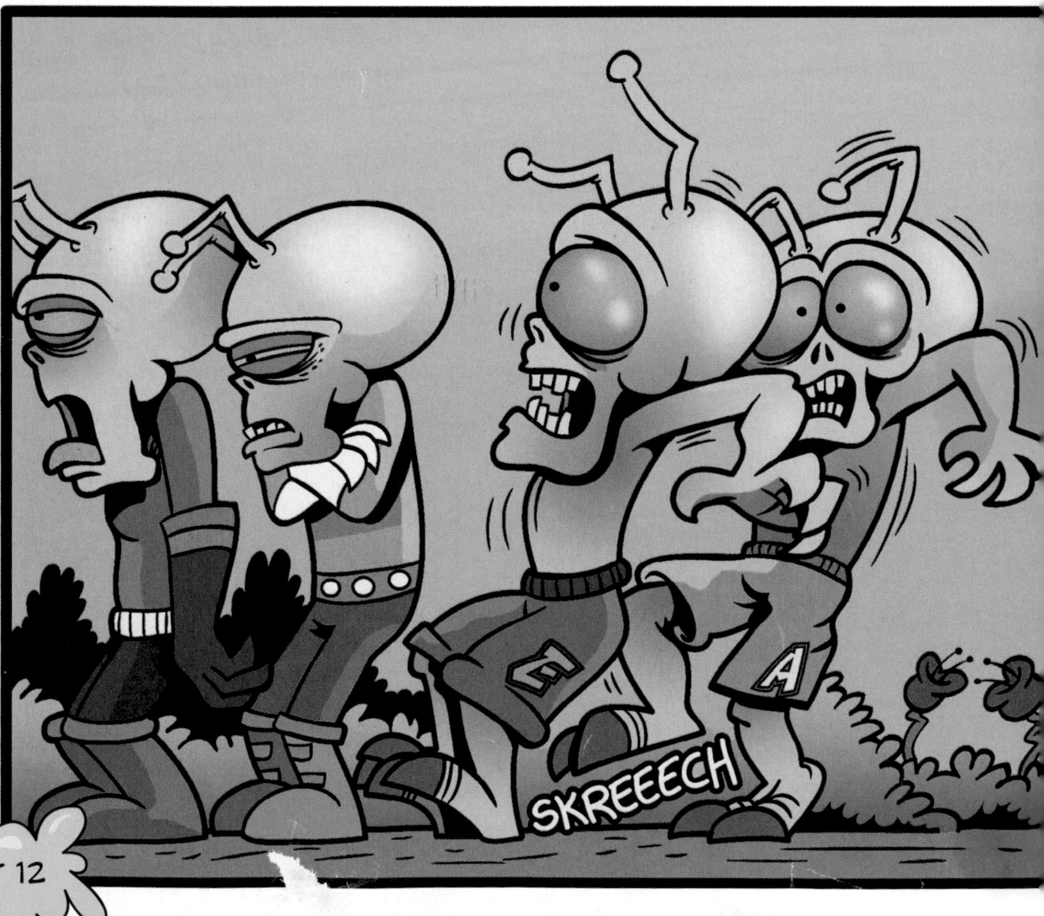
SKREEECH

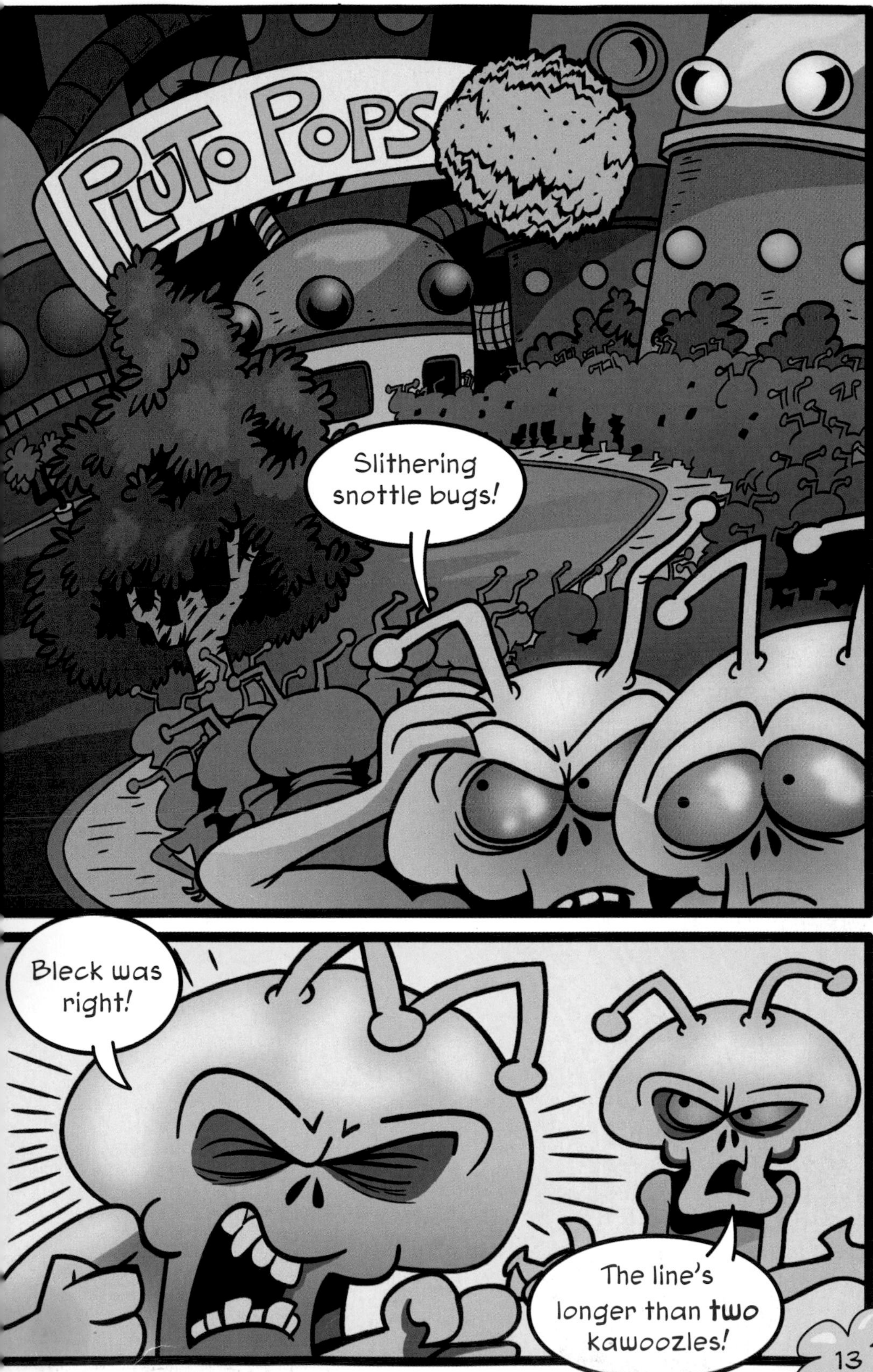
PLUTO POPS
Slithering snottle bugs!
Bleck was right!
The line's longer than **two** kawoozles!

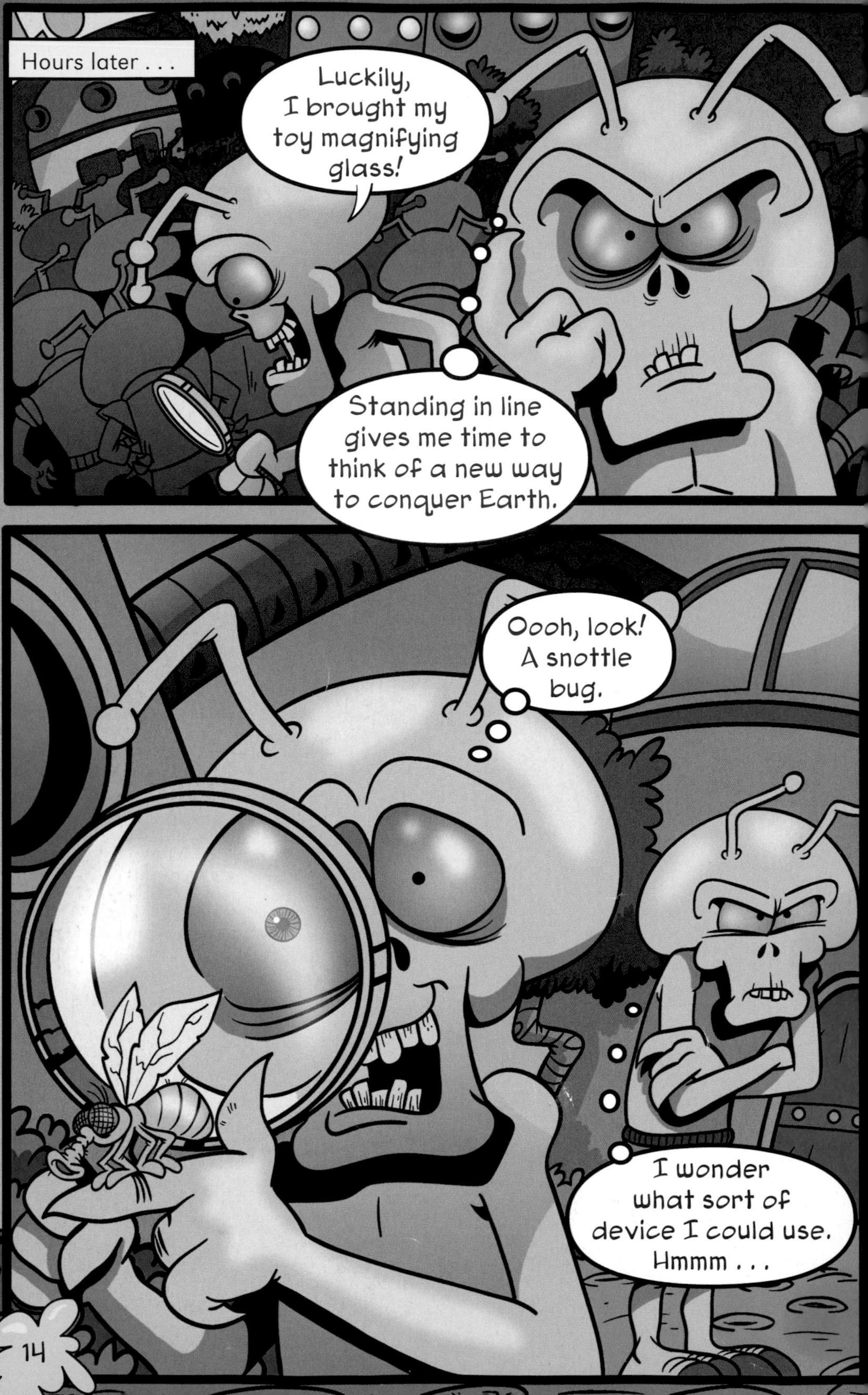
Hours later . . .
Luckily, I brought my toy magnifying glass!
Standing in line gives me time to think of a new way to conquer Earth.
Oooh, look! A snottle bug.
I wonder what sort of device I could use. Hmmm . . .

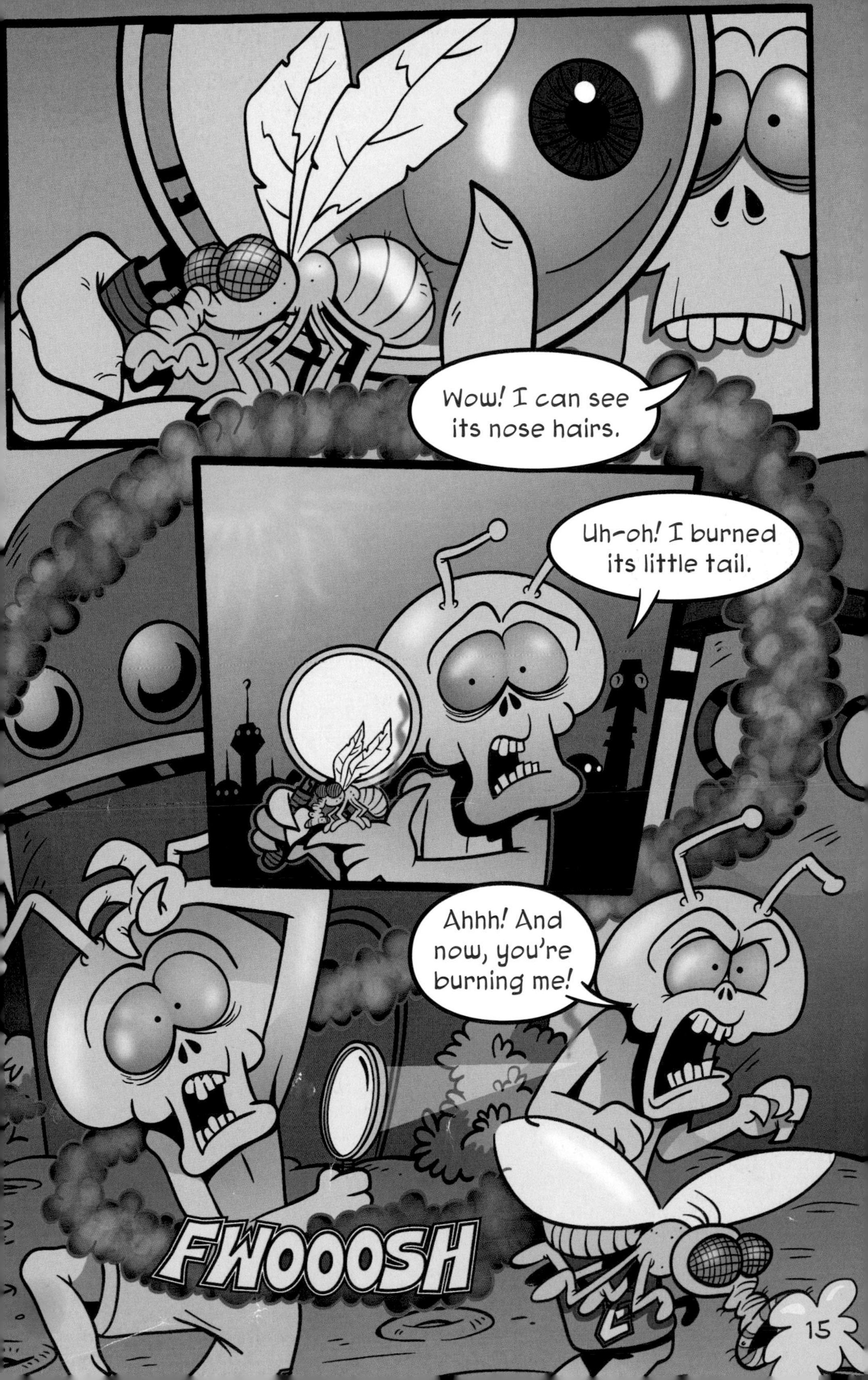
Wow! I can see its nose hairs.
Uh-oh! I burned its little tail.
Ahhh! And now, you're burning me!
FWOOOSH

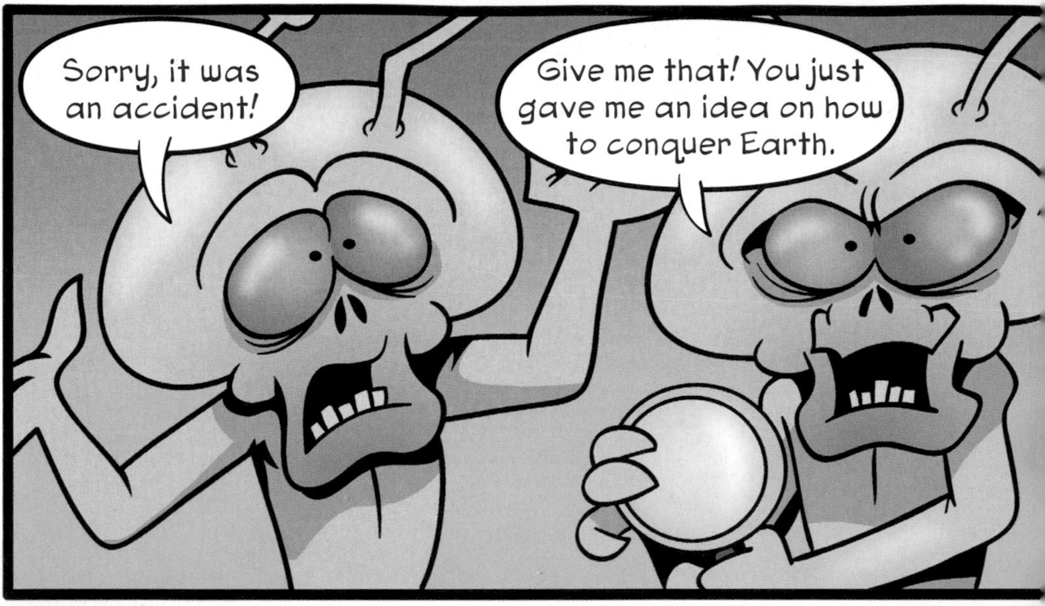
Sorry, it was an accident!
Give me that! You just gave me an idea on how to conquer Earth.

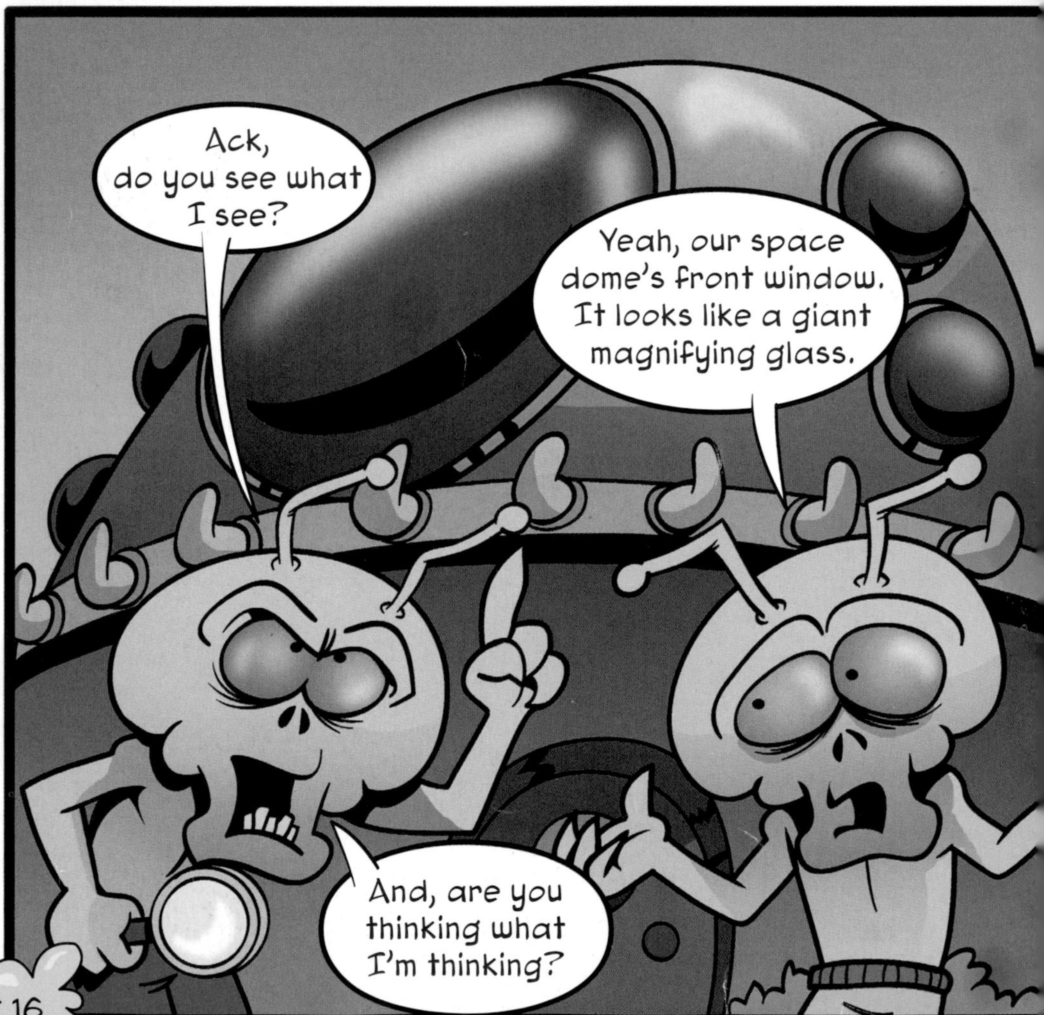
Ack, do you see what I see?
Yeah, our space dome's front window. It looks like a giant magnifying glass.
And, are you thinking what I'm thinking?

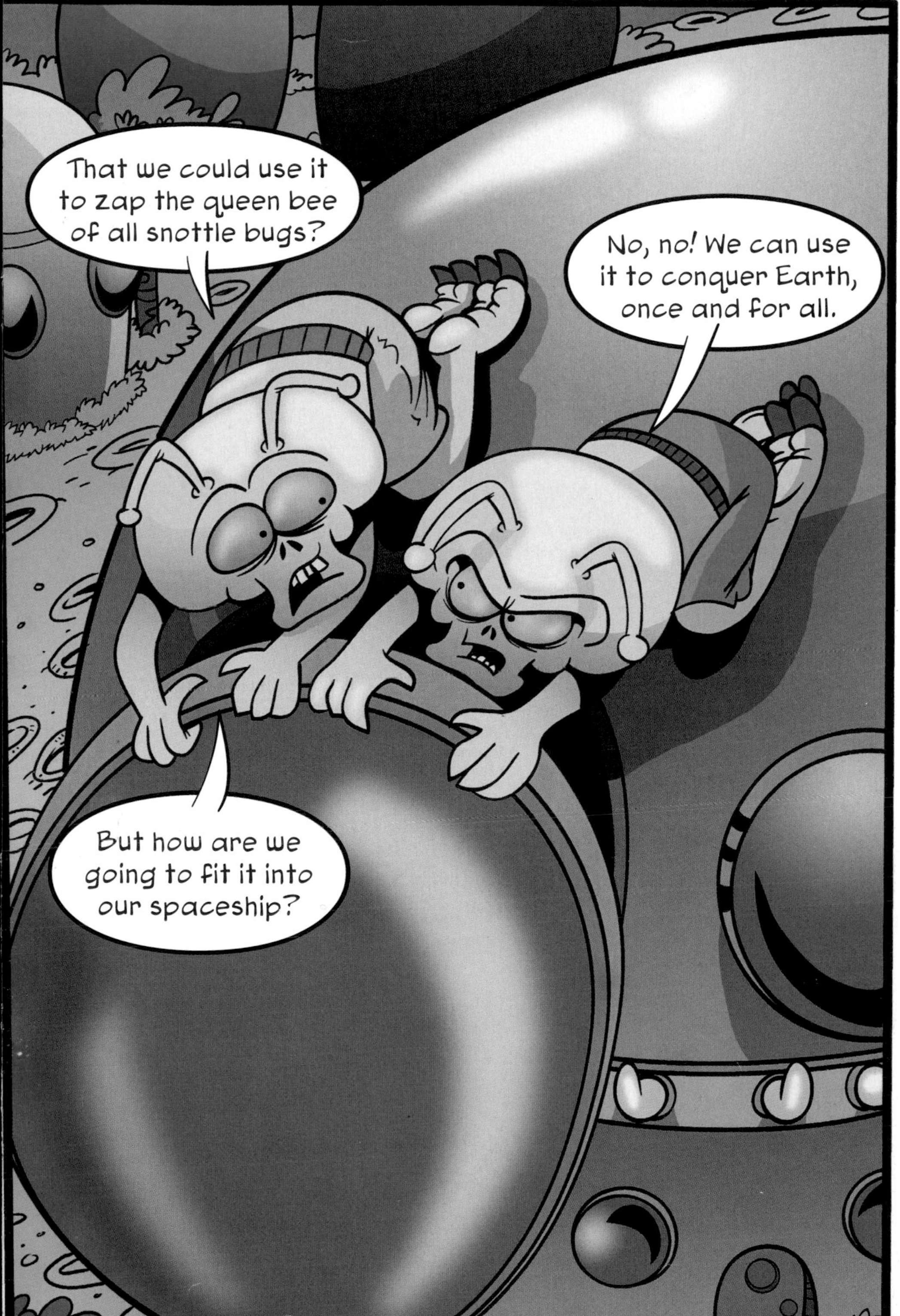
That we could use it to zap the queen bee of all snottle bugs?
No, no! We can use it to conquer Earth, once and for all.
But how are we going to fit it into our spaceship?

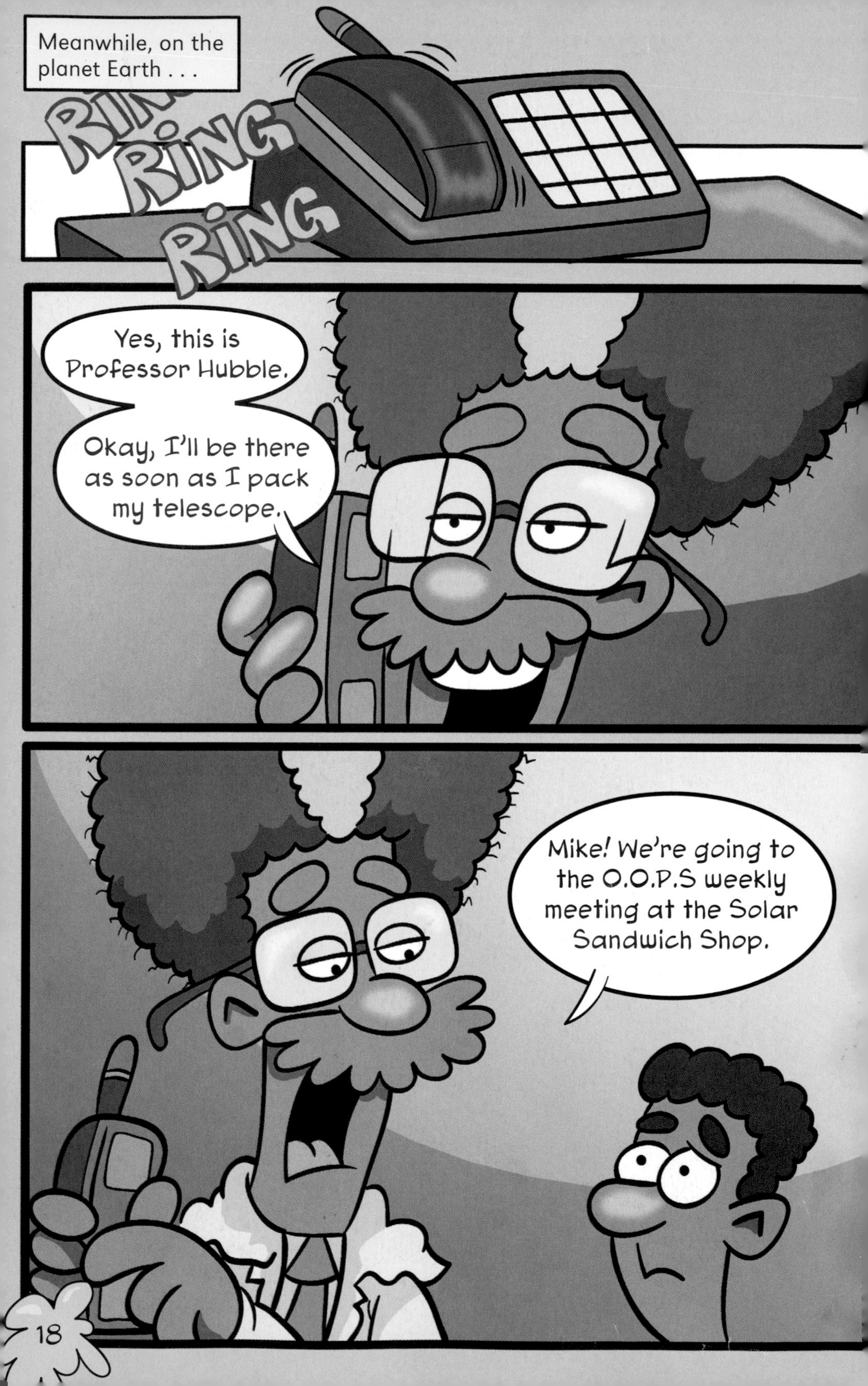
Meanwhile, on the planet Earth . . .
RING RING RING
Yes, this is Professor Hubble.
Okay, I'll be there as soon as I pack my telescope.
Mike! We're going to the O.O.P.S weekly meeting at the Solar Sandwich Shop.

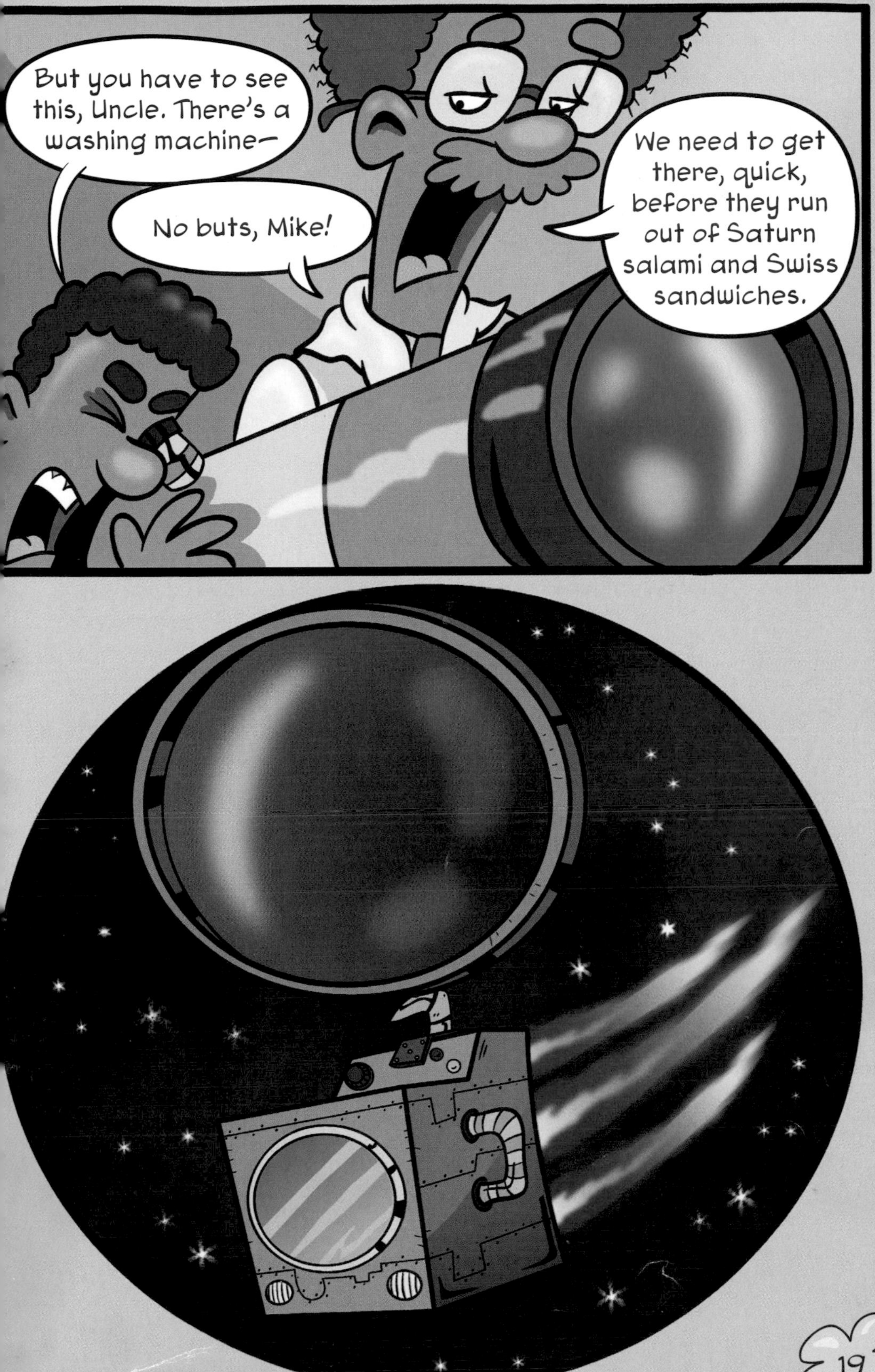
But you have to see this, Uncle. There's a washing machine—
No buts, Mike!
We need to get there, quick, before they run out of Saturn salami and Swiss sandwiches.

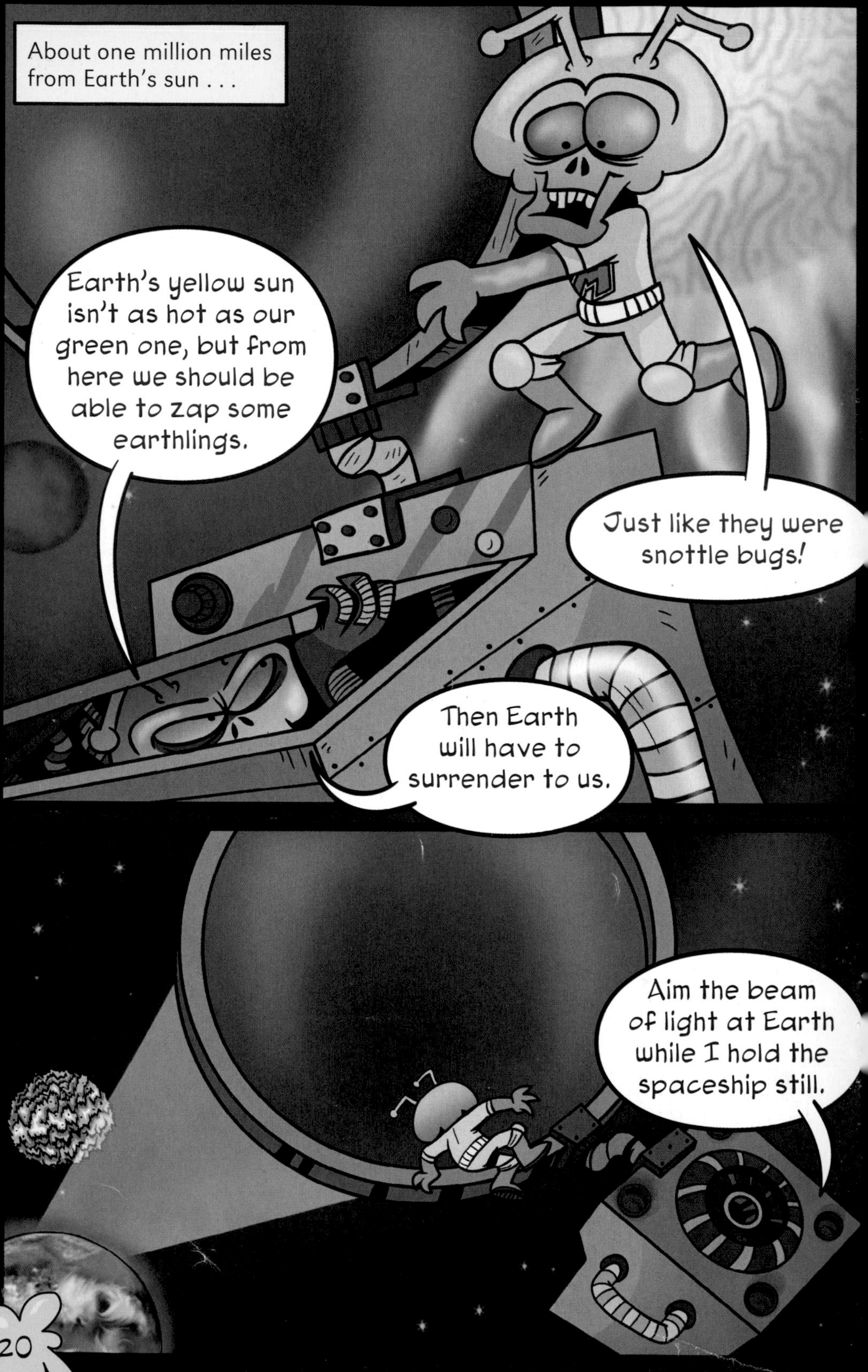

About one million miles from Earth's sun . . .
Earth's yellow sun isn't as hot as our green one, but from here we should be able to zap some earthlings.
Just like they were snottle bugs!
Then Earth will have to surrender to us.
Aim the beam of light at Earth while I hold the spaceship still.

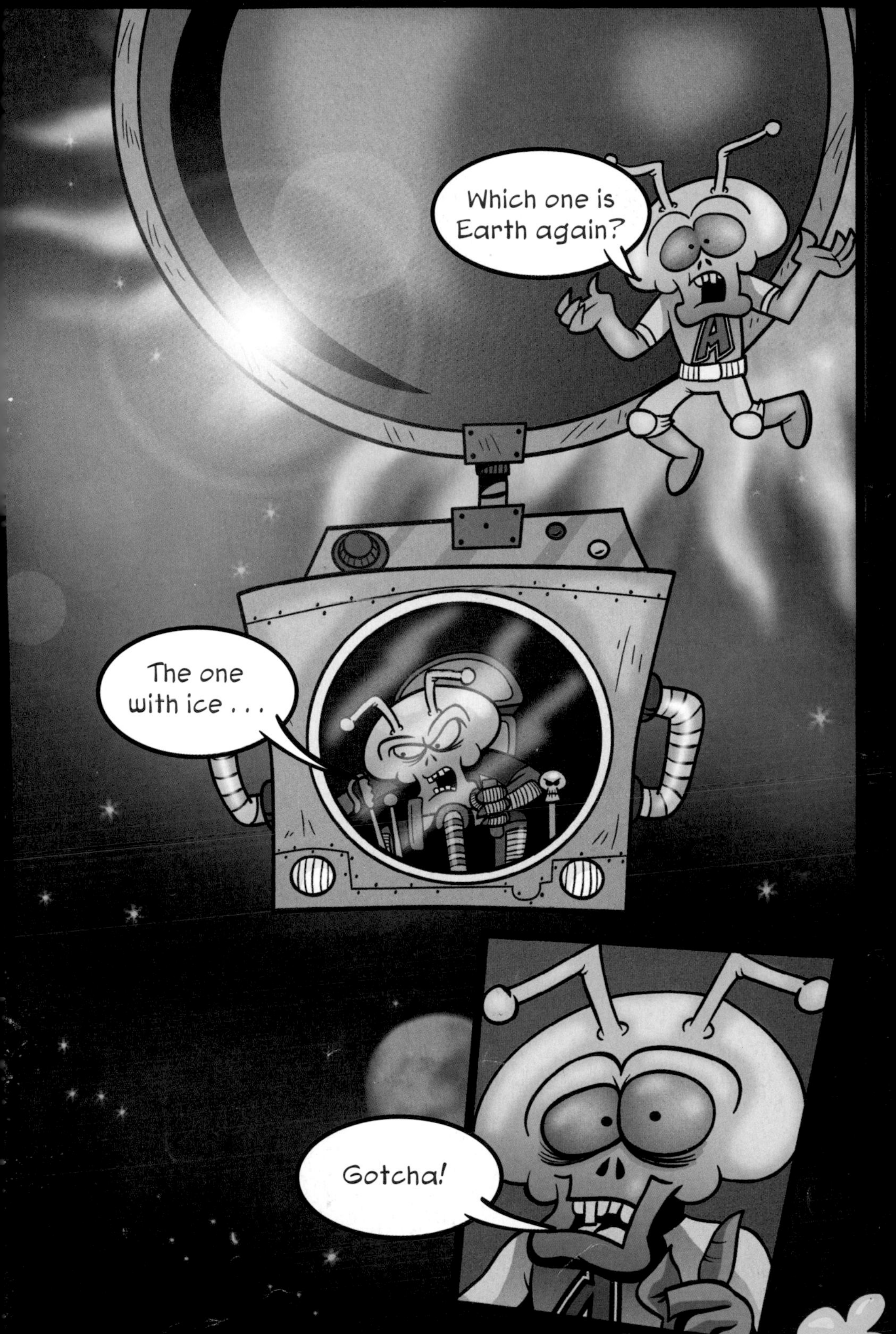
Which one is Earth again?
The one with ice . . .
Gotcha!

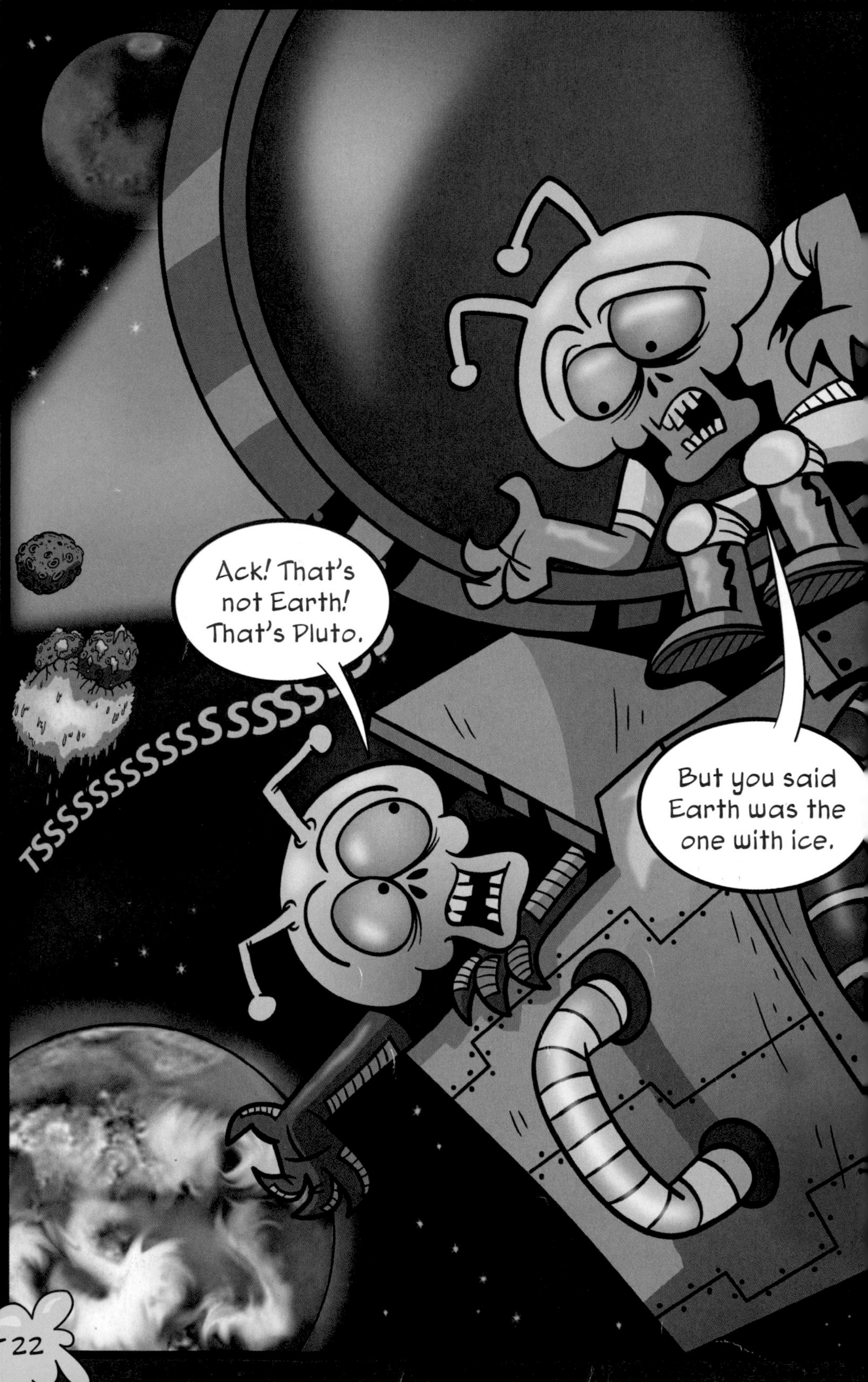
Ack! That's not Earth! That's Pluto.
But you said Earth was the one with ice.
TSSSSSSSSSSSSSSS

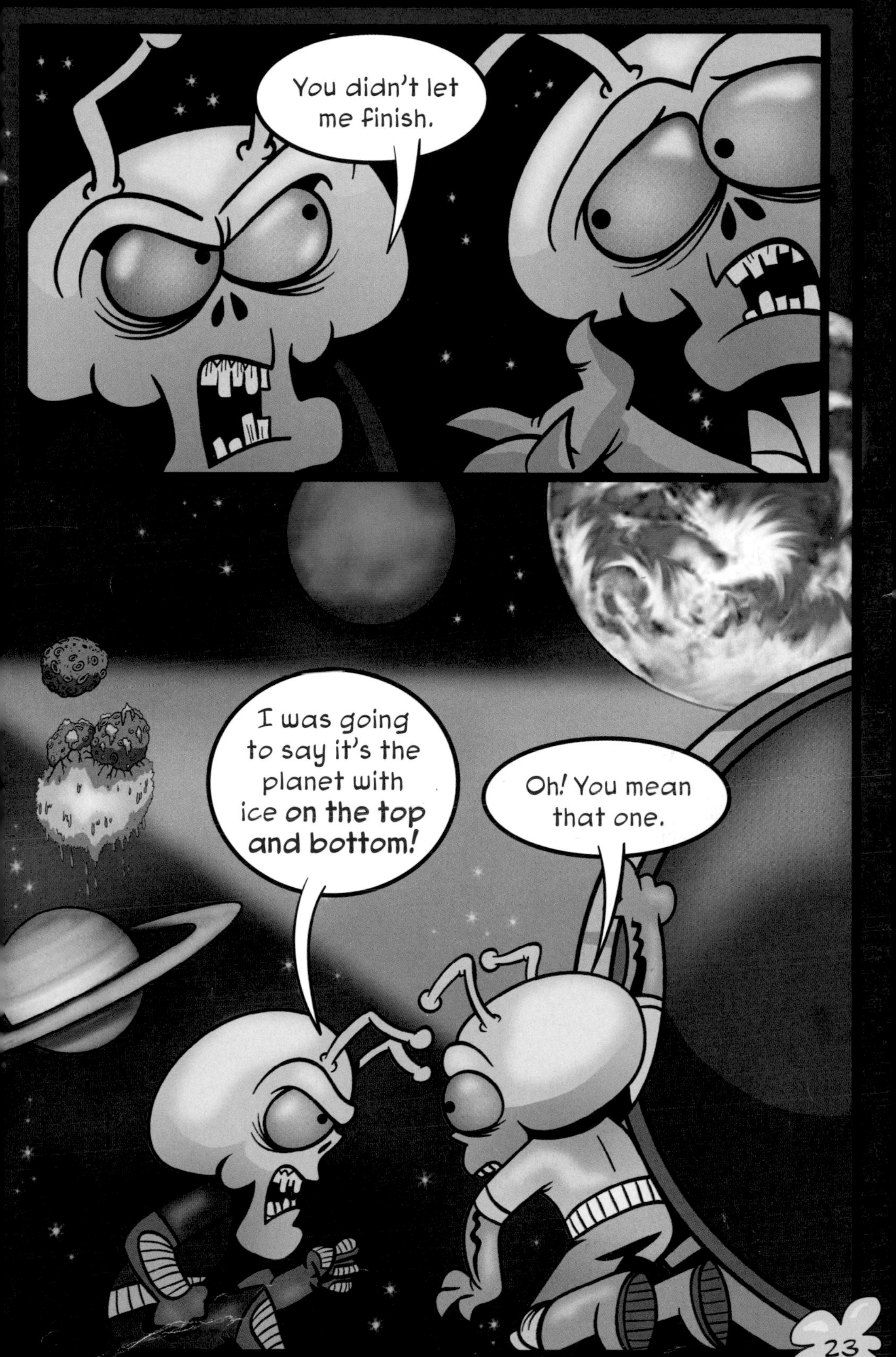
You didn't let me finish.
I was going to say it's the planet with ice on the top and bottom!
Oh! You mean that one.

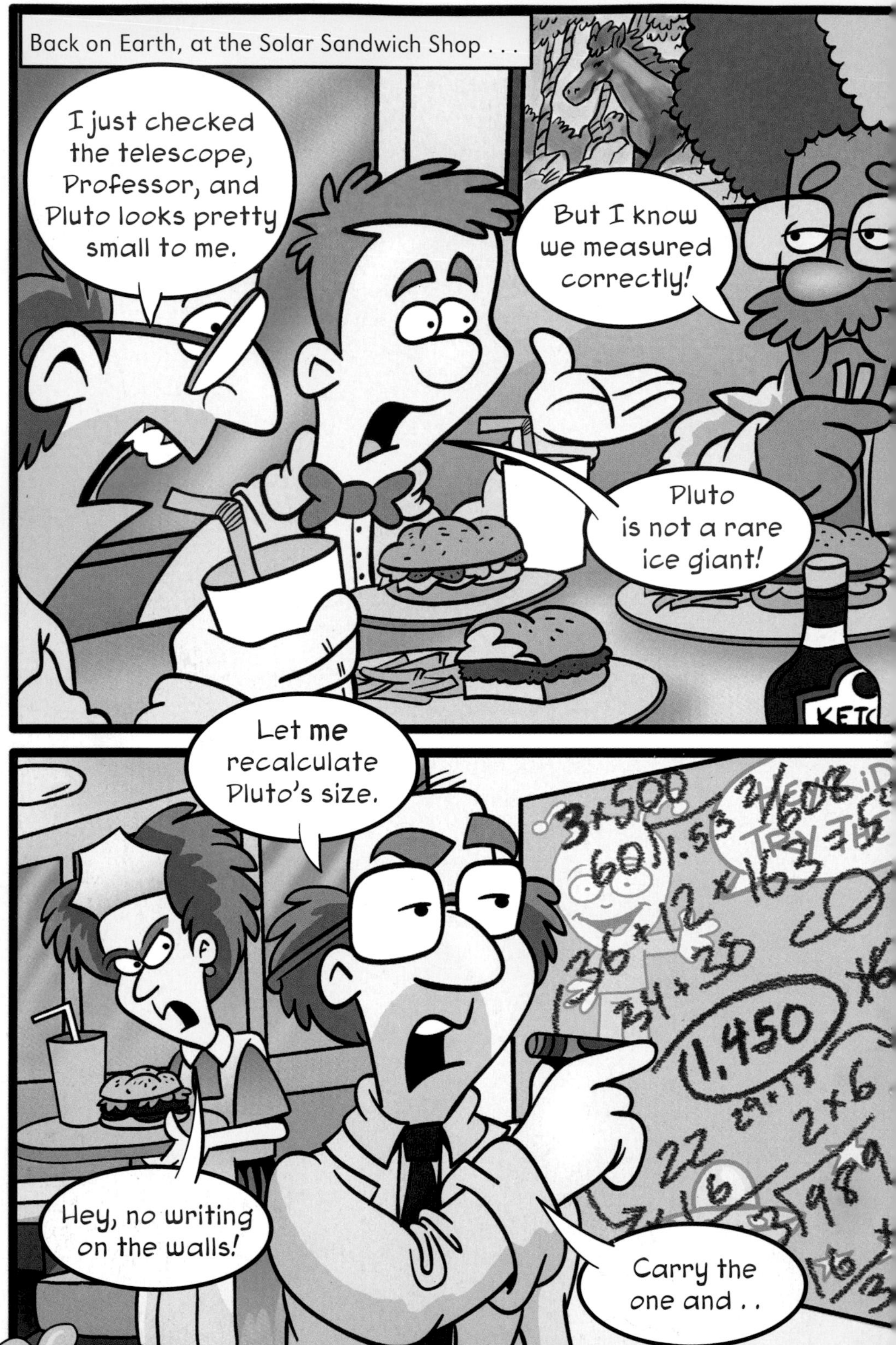
Back on Earth, at the Solar Sandwich Shop . . .
I just checked the telescope, Professor, and Pluto looks pretty small to me.
But I know we measured correctly!
Pluto is not a rare ice giant!
Let me recalculate Pluto's size.
Hey, no writing on the walls!
Carry the one and . .

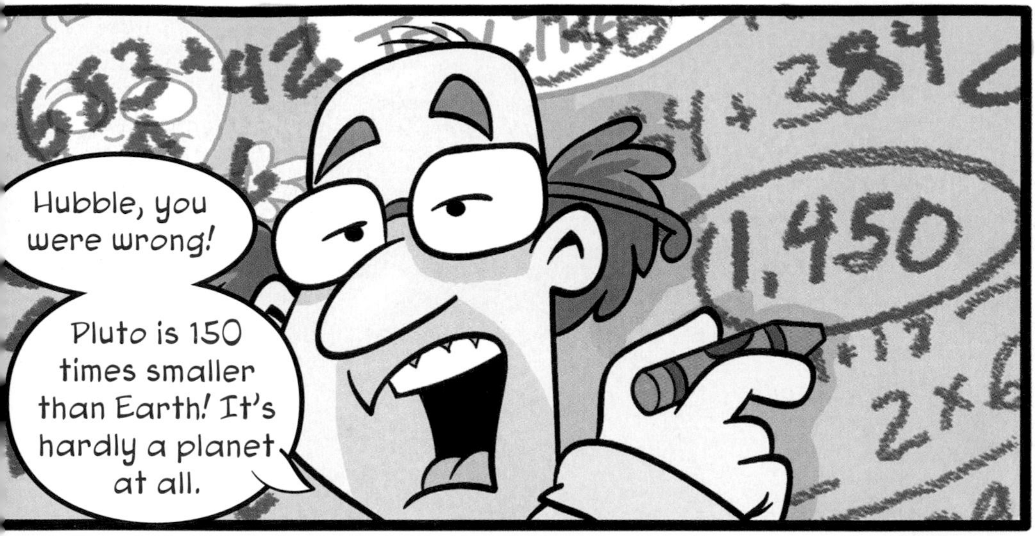
683*42
1,450
Hubble, you were wrong!
Pluto is 150 times smaller than Earth! It's hardly a planet at all.

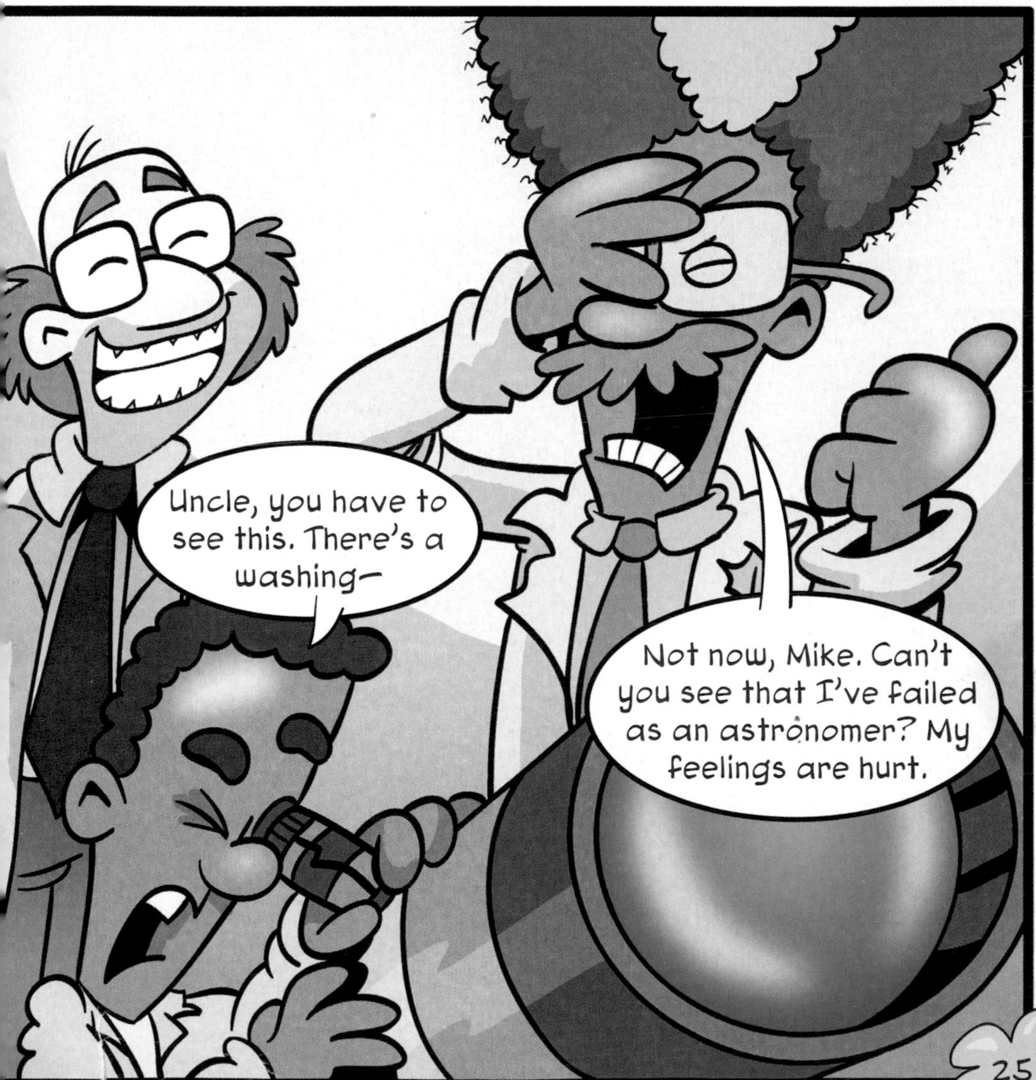
Uncle, you have to see this. There's a washing—
Not now, Mike. Can't you see that I've failed as an astronomer? My feelings are hurt.

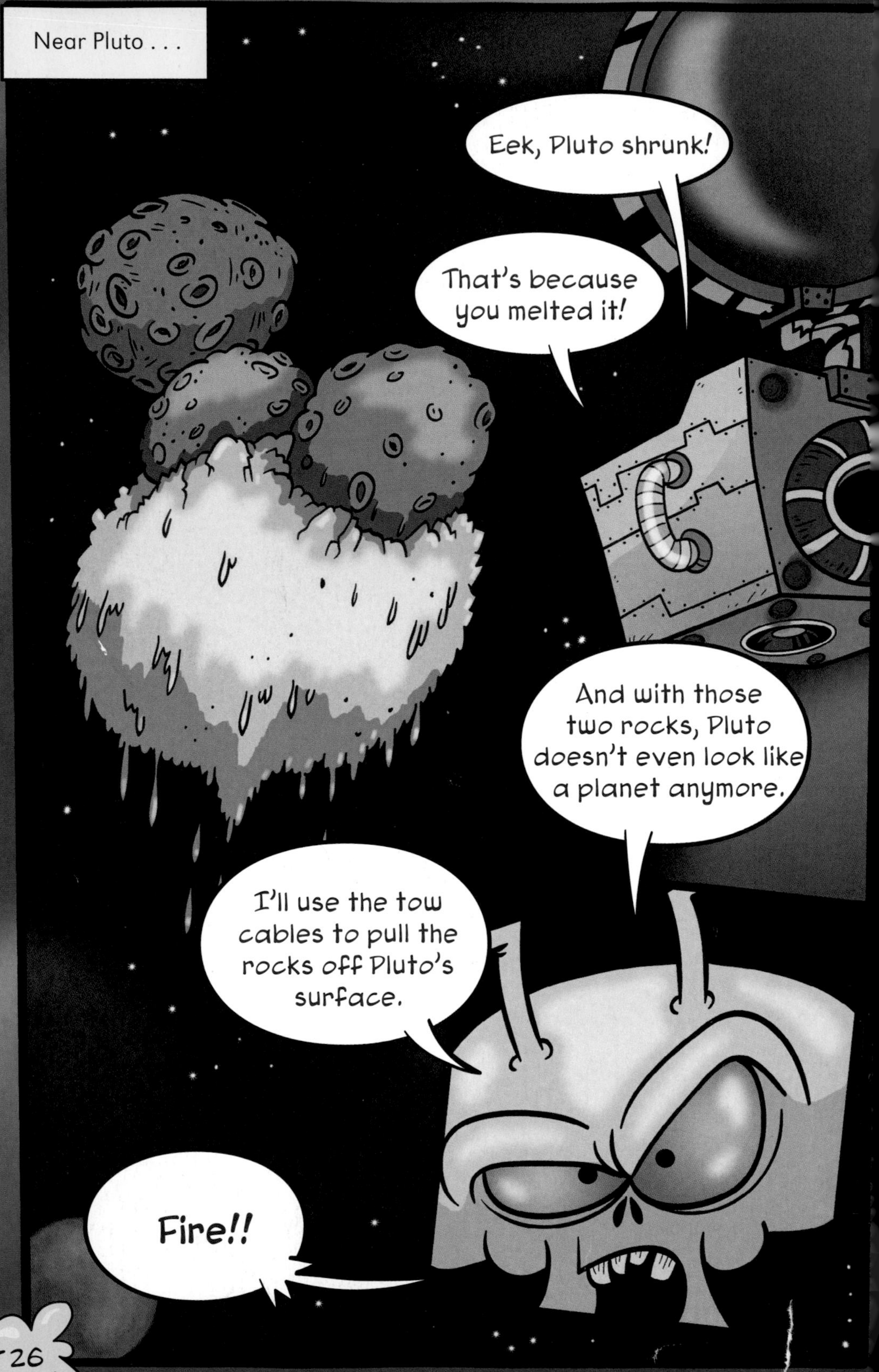
Near Pluto . . .
Eek, Pluto shrunk!
That's because you melted it!
And with those two rocks, Pluto doesn't even look like a planet anymore.
I'll use the tow cables to pull the rocks off Pluto's surface.
Fire!!

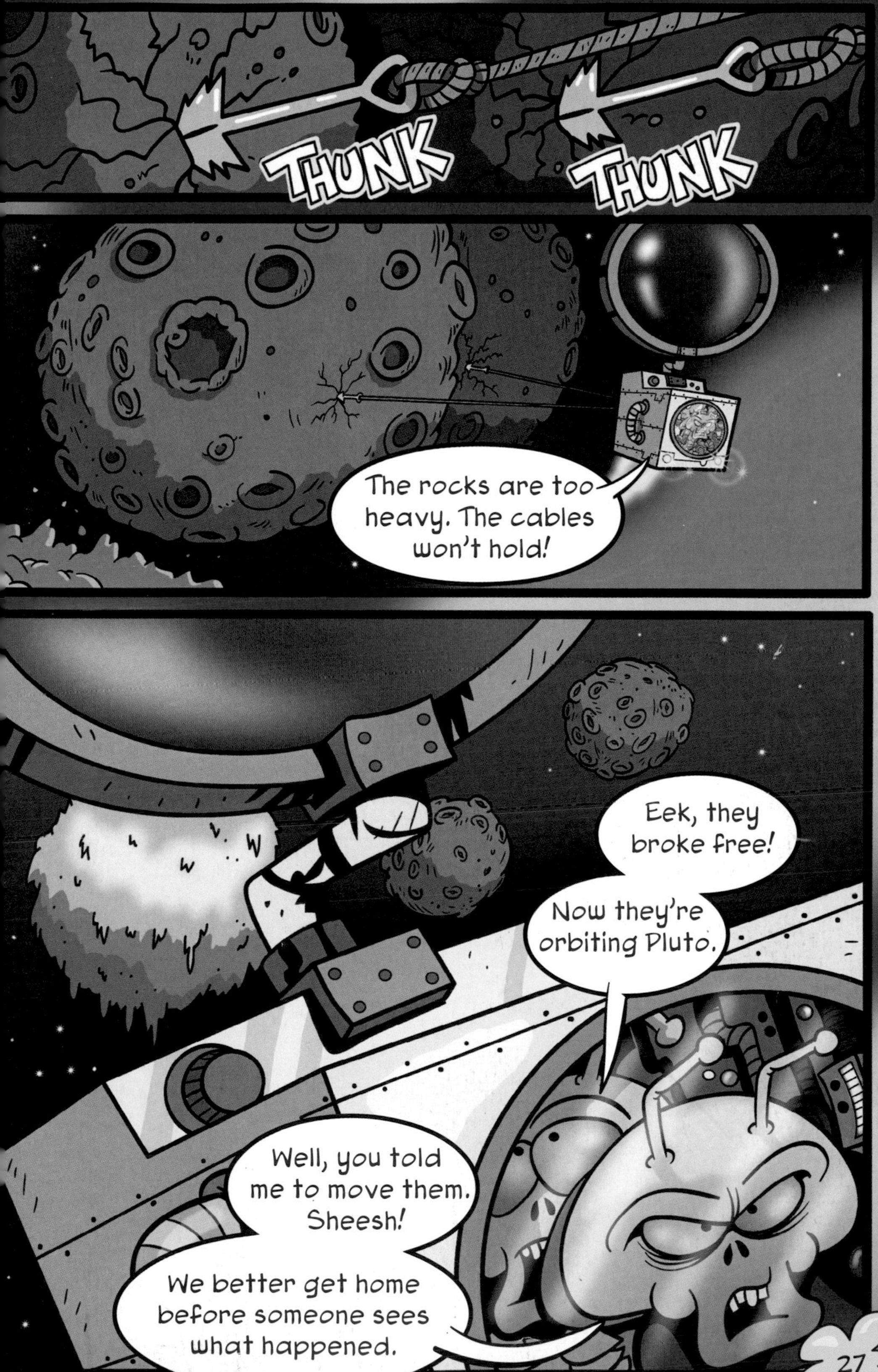
THUNK
THUNK
The rocks are too heavy. The cables won't hold!
Eek, they broke free!
Now they're orbiting Pluto.
Well, you told me to move them. Sheesh!
We better get home before someone sees what happened.

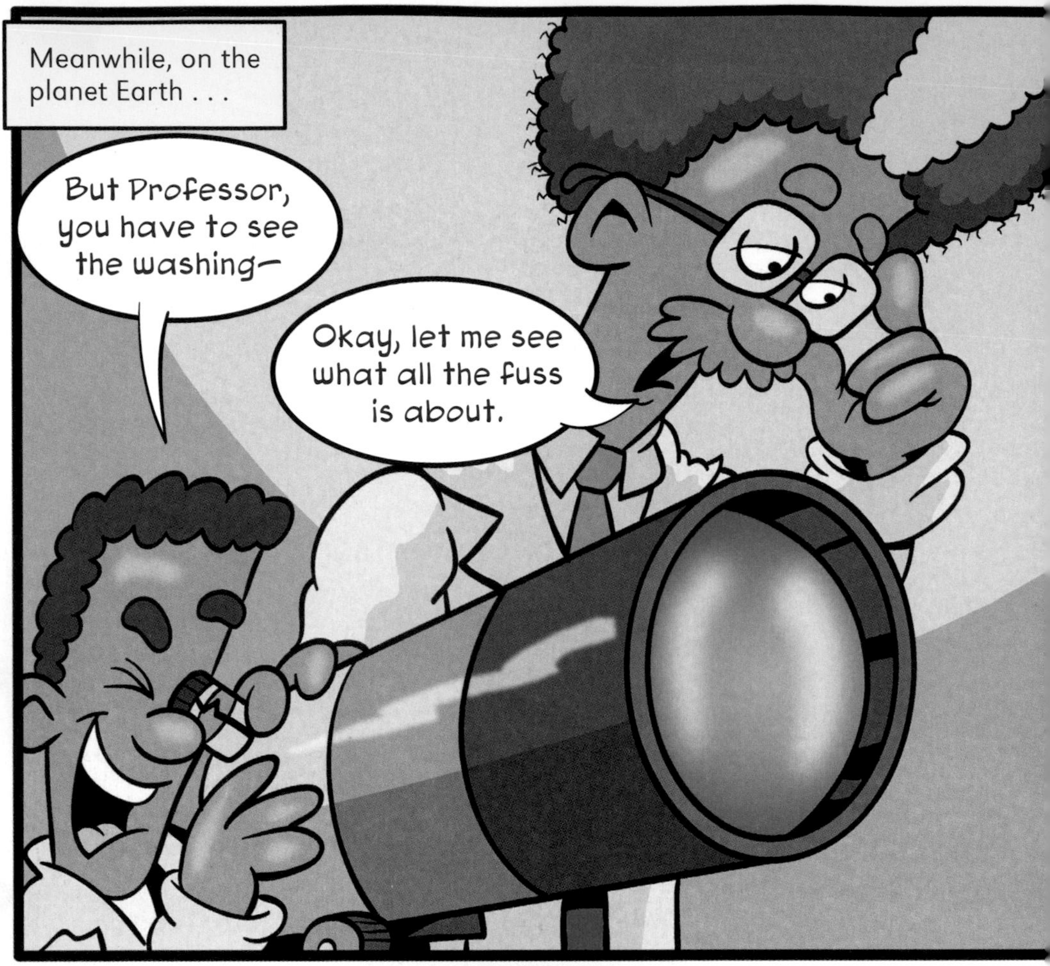
Meanwhile, on the planet Earth . . .
But Professor, you have to see the washing—
Okay, let me see what all the fuss is about.

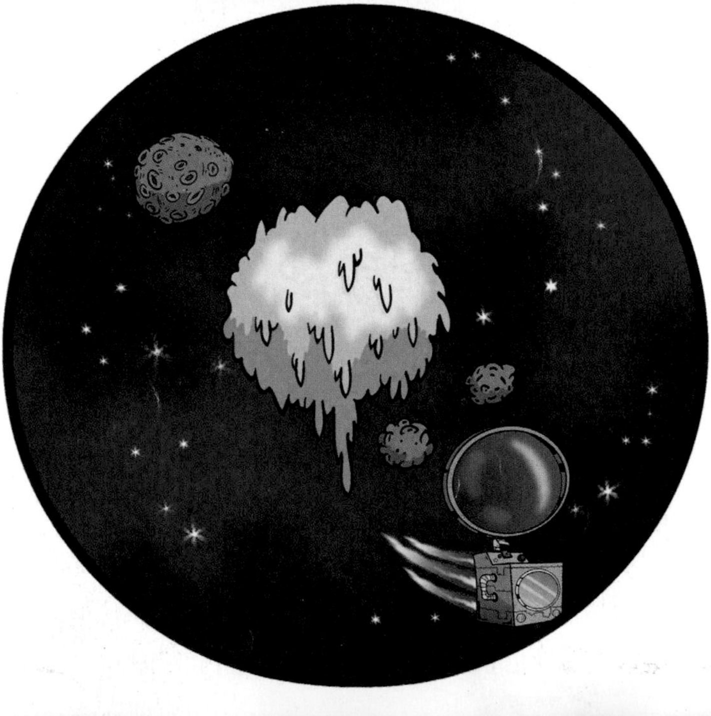

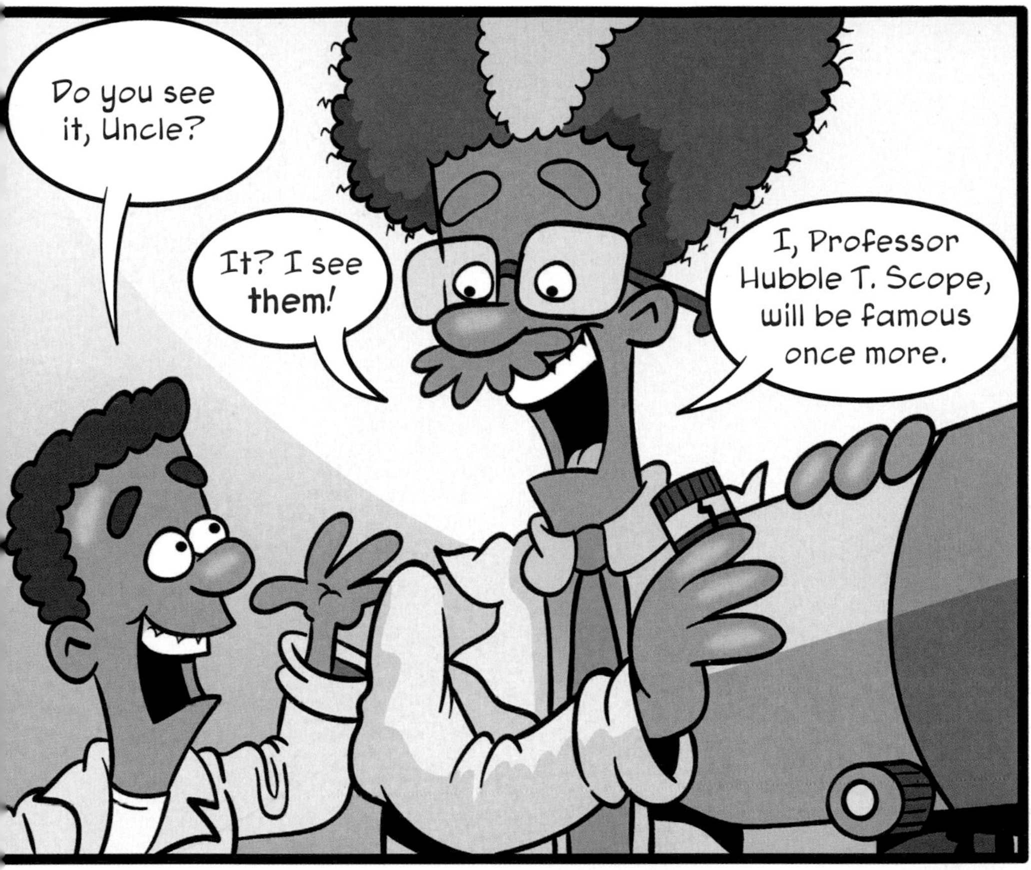
Do you see it, Uncle?
It? I see **them**!
I, Professor Hubble T. Scope, will be famous once more.

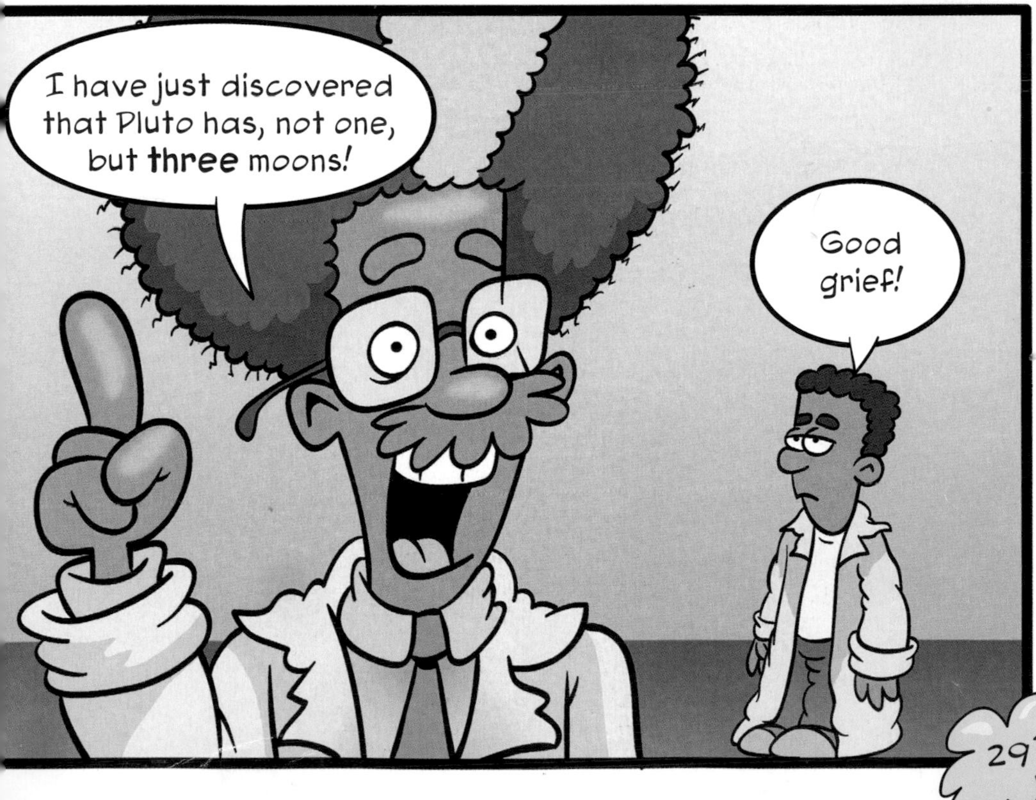
I have just discovered that Pluto has, not one, but **three** moons!
Good grief!

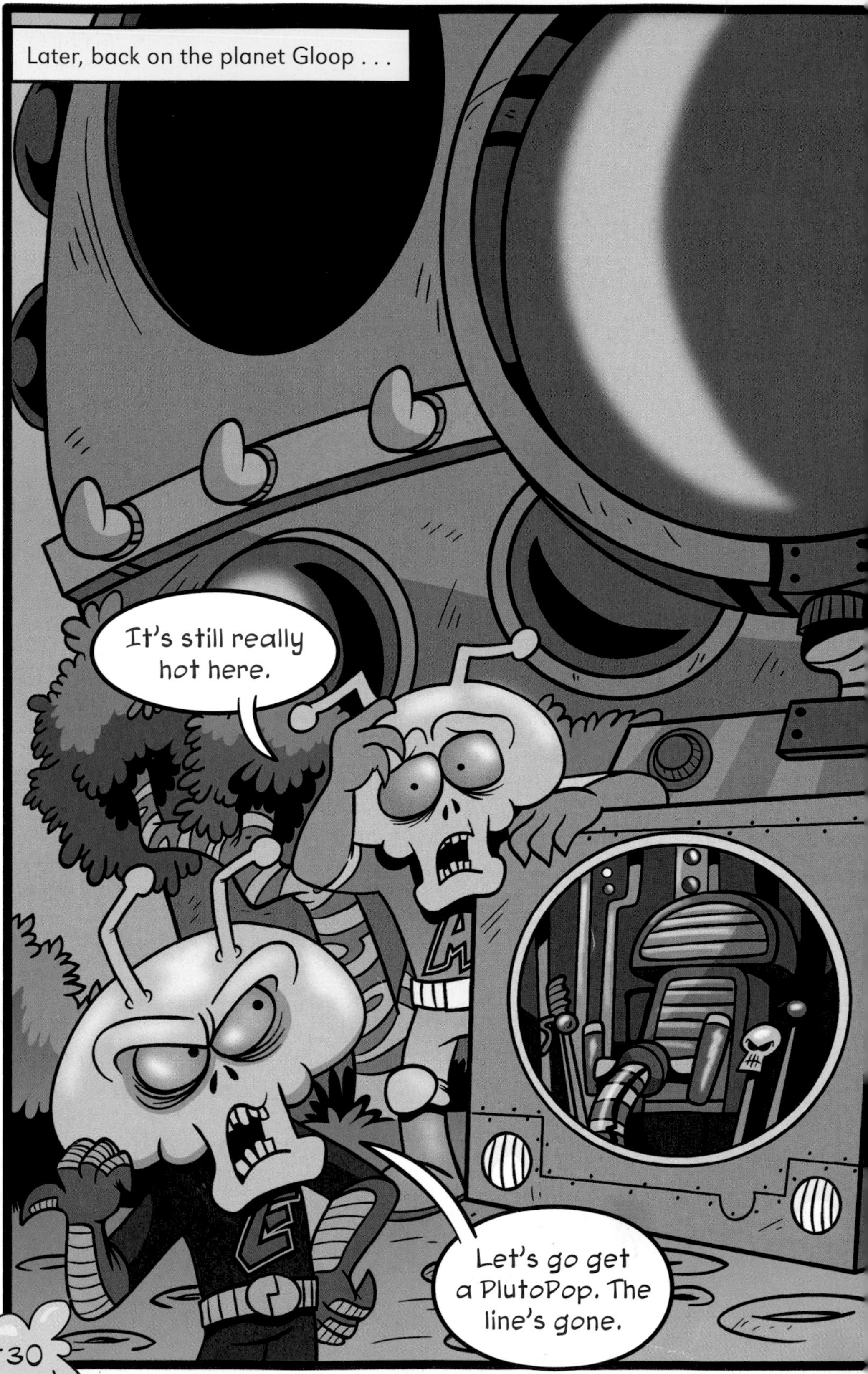
Later, back on the planet Gloop . . .
It's still really hot here.
Let's go get a PlutoPop. The line's gone.

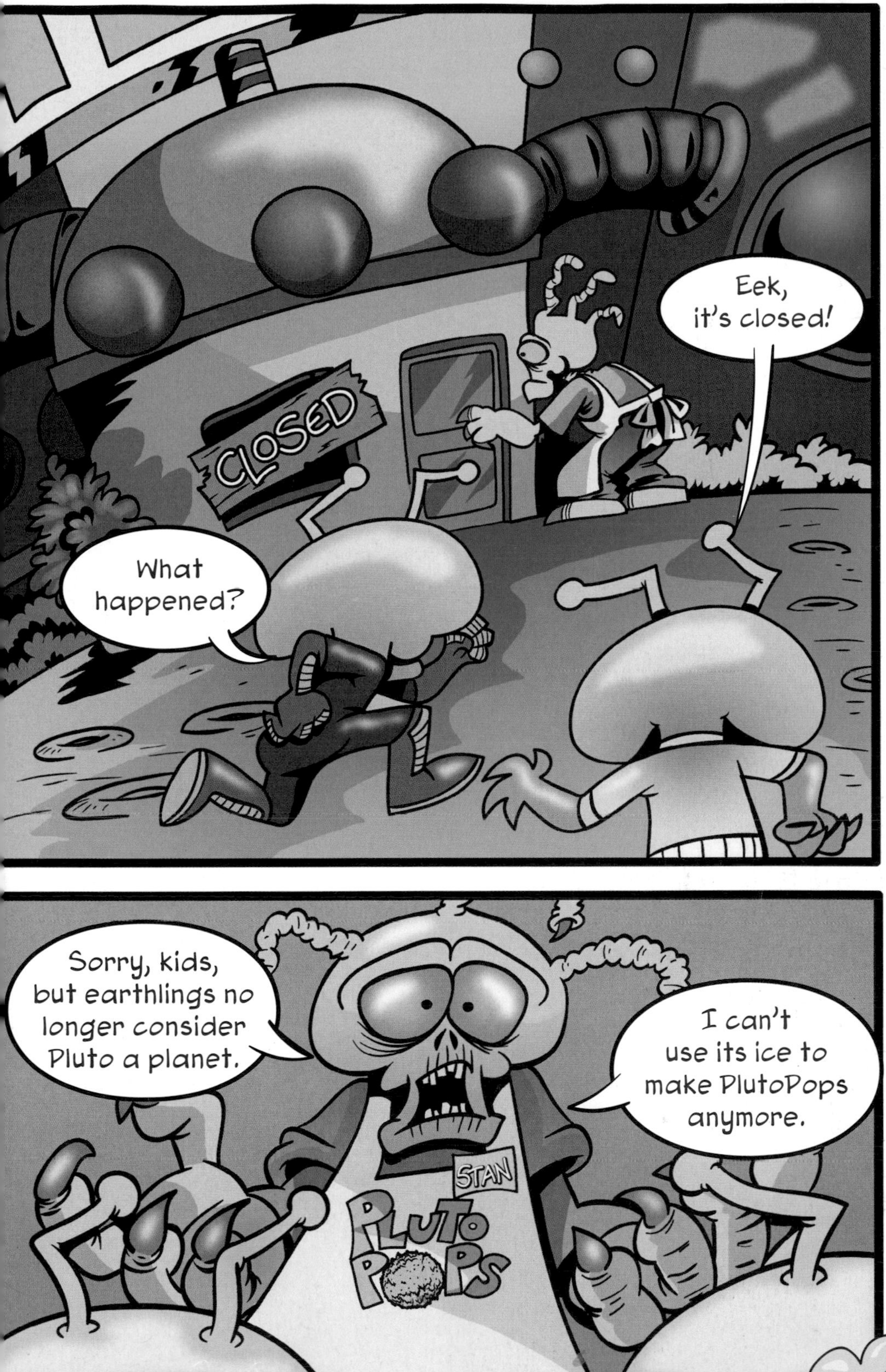
CLOSED
Eek, it's closed!
What happened?
Sorry, kids, but earthlings no longer consider Pluto a planet.
I can't use its ice to make PlutoPops anymore.
STAN
PLUTO POPS

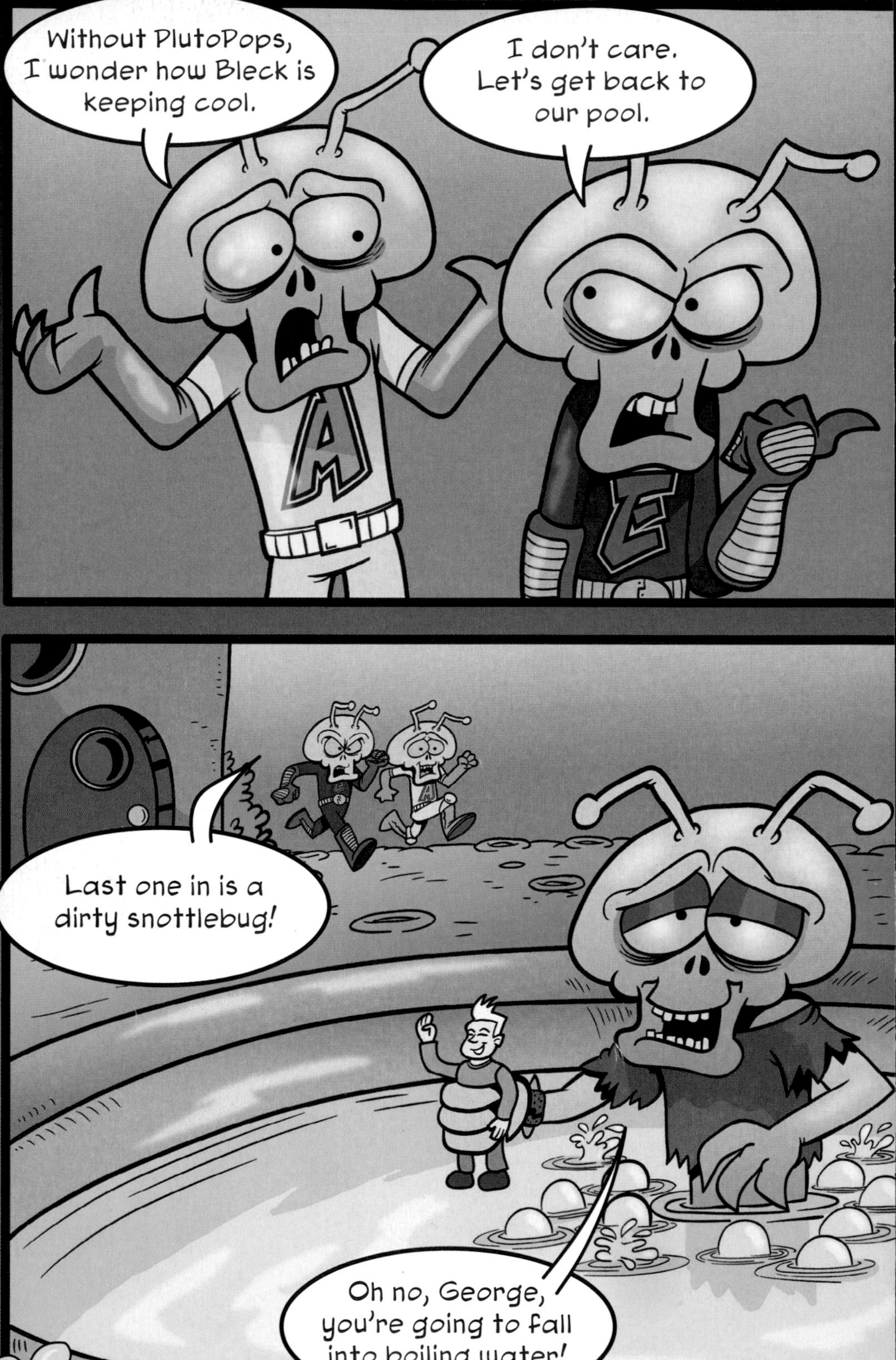
Without PlutoPops, I wonder how Bleck is keeping cool.
I don't care. Let's get back to our pool.
Last one in is a dirty snottlebug!
Oh no, George, you're going to fall into boiling water!

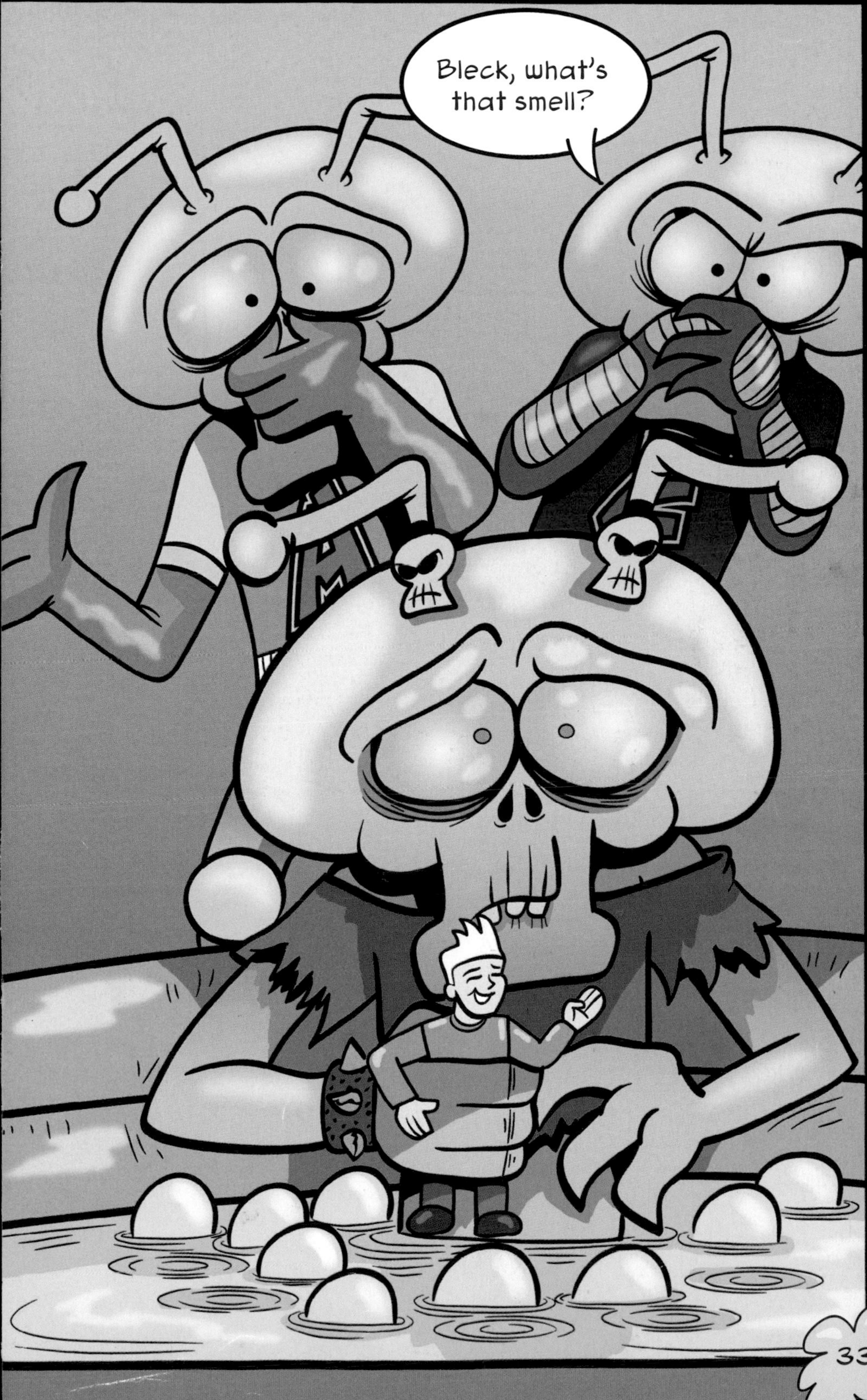
Bleck, what's that smell?

ABOUT THE AUTHOR

Blake A. Hoena once spent a whole weekend just watching his favorite science-fiction movies. Those movies made him wonder what kind of aliens, with their death rays and hyper-drives, couldn't actually conquer Earth. That's when he created Eek and Ack, who play at conquering Earth like earthling kids play at stopping bad guys. Blake has written more than 20 books for children, and currently lives in Minneapolis, Minnesota.

ABOUT THE ILLUSTRATOR

Steve Harpster has loved to draw funny cartoons, mean monsters, and goofy gadgets since he was able to pick up a pencil. In first grade, he avoided writing assignments by working on the pictures for stories instead. Steve was able to land a job drawing funny pictures for books, and that's really what he's best at. Steve lives in Columbus, Ohio, with his wonderful wife, Karen, and their sheepdog, Doodle.

 GLOSSARY

action figures (AK-shuhn FIG-yurz)—toys that boys play with; some people mistake them for dolls, but they're not dolls!

astronomer (uh-STRON-uh-muhr)—a scientist who spends a lot of time studying planets, stars, and other stuff in outer space

Einstein (EYEN-styn)—one of the few earthlings that Gloopers (people from the planet Gloop) consider smart

kawoozle (kah-WOOZ-uhl)—a very long, thin creature that lives on the planet Gloop; kawoozles have a body like a snake, but instead of scales, they have sponge-like skin, which picks up dirt and mud as they crawl along the ground, thus the saying "dirty kawoozle". Kawoozles can grow to be an Earth-mile long.

sinister plot (SIN-uh-stur PLOT)—an evil plan, such as zapping earthlings with a giant magnifying glass

telescope (TEL-uh-skope)—an instrument that makes things that are far away look closer and larger, such as stars, planets, and flying washing machines, um, we mean spaceships

FACTS FROM BEYOND

American astronomer Clyde Tombaugh discovered Pluto in 1930.

Eleven-year-old Venetia Burney from Great Britain suggested that Tombaugh's discovery be called Pluto, after the Roman god of the Underworld.

Charon (KARE-on), Pluto's largest moon, was discovered in 1978 by American astronomer James Christy. Its smaller moons, Nix and Hydra, were discovered in 2005 with the Hubble Space Telescope.

Pluto is now called a dwarf planet. Astronomers consider Pluto a dwarf planet because of its small size, and because it shares an orbit with other large objects, such as asteroids. True planets don't share their orbits with other large objects.

All of the research on Pluto has been performed using telescopes. The Hubble Space Telescope was launched in 1990. It has helped astronomers learn even more about Pluto.

NASA launched *New Horizons* in 2006. This spacecraft is expected to reach Pluto in 2015.

PLUTO STATS

- One Pluto year equals 249 Earth years.

- One Pluto day equals 6 Earth days.

- Pluto's surface temperature is minus 391 degrees Fahrenheit. It's so cold that oxygen on Pluto is frozen solid!

- Pluto's diameter is about 1,450 miles across.

- Pluto is about 150 times smaller than Earth.

- Pluto is only 2/3 the size of Earth's moon.

DISCUSSION QUESTIONS

1. Pluto is round like a planet. It has moons like a planet. Scientists, though, now call it a dwarf planet. What do you think? Should Pluto still be considered a planet? Why or why not?

2. Eek and Ack have different ideas about what they could use a giant magnifying glass for. Eek wants to use it to conquer Earth, and Ack wants to zap the queen bee of all snottle bugs. How are Eek and Ack different and how are they similar? Use examples from the story to explain your answers.

3. How would you conquer Earth if you were Eek and Ack?

WRITING PROMPTS

1. The author uses Eek and Ack to explain why Pluto is no longer considered a planet. They shrunk it! Write a fictional story explaining why something else in our solar system is the way that it is. For example, why is Mars red or why does Saturn have rings?

2. Imagine that astronomers discovered a new planet in our solar system. Describe this new planet. Don't forget to introduce who discovered it and mention where it can be found.

3. In the story, Mike helps his uncle Hubble with his work. Do your parents or one of your relatives have a job that you would like to help them with? Write why, and describe what it would be like helping them for a day.

INTERNET SITES

The book may be over, but the adventure is just beginning.

Do you want to read more about the subjects or ideas in this book? Want to play cool games or watch videos about the authors who write these books? Then go to FactHound. At *www.facthound.com*, you'll be able to do all that, and more. The FactHound website can also send you to other safe Internet sites.

Check it out!